The Neon Rose

Published by bluechrome publishing 2007

2 4 6 8 10 9 7 5 3 1

First published in Great Britain in 2007 by
bluechrome publishing
PO Box 109,
Portishead, Bristol. BS20 7ZJ

www.bluechrome.co.uk

A CIP catalogue record for this book is available from the
British Library.

ISBN 978-1-906061-07-4

Printed by Biddles Ltd, King's Lynn, Norfolk

The Neon Rose

Fred Johnston

Author Note

The following story was inspired, if that is not too vulgar a word, by having met, too briefly, a young Irishman begging on his knees on the rue de Rivoli in Paris. I am grateful to a number of people for having made room in which I might write this book; in particular to Judith and Géraldine at the Princess Grace Irish Library at Monaco, where I had a lovely time and a creative time; to Maryvonne Boisseau, at Poitiers; to the management and staff of the Hotel Beauséjour in Paris, who were always so kind and helpful when I stayed there; to Annie Semmau, courageous Corsican, inspiring poet and photographer and friend in Paris; to Kristian Ar Braz; and my thanks also to the Arts Council of Ireland (Dublin) for their support; and others who, unforgivably, have slipped my mind.

{*Galway-Monaco-Nantes: August 28th 2005*}

- to Sylvia, with love

"…..like the make-believe of a child who is remaking the world, not always in the same way; but always after his own heart."

- W.B. Yeats: *Ideas of Good and Evil* (Macmillan, 1903)

The First Day

Il m'a dit:

His body was not in the studio. You know that, where I found it. It was at the bottom of the stairs up to his bedroom. There was a lot of blood. All around his head. Here and there. Like a dark red shining halo. At first I didn't know who it was. I leaned over him. Then I called the police. The studio, again as you know, was across the yard.

Where was the girl?

She was not there. I don't know where she was at that time.

But it was late in the evening. I am told that some people think they should turn up the flagstones in his yard.

That's not funny.

Continue, please.

He was fully dressed when I found him. I smelled wine and thought he was drunk. Then there was the wine bottle on the ground, in pieces.

Blood and wine.

Yet he wondered, couldn't help it, when the young *avocat* left, his lawyer. Whether they'd painted the interview room just for him.

The smell of paint came off the green walls, or perhaps had stayed in his nostrils from the painter's studio; a shadowy square box of paintings half-completed, squeezed tubes of paint, thinners, brushes, books, canvas, photographs, a ruined couch, a massacred table, images trapped in that room and suffocating slightly under the painter's defiant dream, every sitter slammed against a brown background of indistinct hills and curiously gabled towns. This stuffy stuffed room and walled yard which had seen and captured so much, so that it was not unbelievable that the murder of the man was there too, its Borgian *tableau* imprinted in the air, if only some sufficiently sophisticated piece of forensic technology existed that could detect it.

The solitary guard allowed him time to sit and smoke, one cigarette, as if he had all the time in the world. Whether the little nervous *avocat* believed him or not, the story of finding the old man was raggy at best, no longer seemed the point. And the Embassy solicitor, an accent straight out of the moneyed bogs of the Irish midlands, the politically safe bogs, where now and then someone would dig up the half-fossilised remains of an ideal but straight off with it to the museum of such unnecessaries; this man who opened his interview with *I don't know what to say* wasn't helpful. As if he needed help.

He smoked, the guard looked out of the barred Napoleonic window on a stone barracks' square quilted with the leftovers of a recent shower, the heat in the yard matching the heat in the room, he could imagine soft tendrils of steam moving over the Paris pavements.

In the bar, *The Green Roost,* the sign outside a shamrock and the barmen French to the bone, posters on the walls advertising *The Dubliners* and *The Wolfe Tones* – no historic irony intended – and *The Bhoys of Bluehill* – three French students who could barely speak English let alone Irish and who played every Monday evening and no-one listened, he'd been in the pub so often he knew the way the crowds worked; then, over the *Hommes,* a framed reproduction of the 1916 Proclamation and over the piss-drain, ancient acid-spotted posters for Guinness delivered from horse drawn carts, you could buy a copy of the *Irish Independent* from behind the bar, the TV was tuned snowily to Irish TV and *The Sunday Game* had the place rocking: in here, in this transported plastic comes-in-a-kit Irishness he'd met the Jew, well, the half-Yid, brought up in England, traces of a posh accent, and at first he thought the great white face with its absurd frame of thin tinselly red beard and the splotch of flat dyed red hair wanted his body. At the back of the man's head, how could you not notice him yet no one seemed to, like something dropped from the ceiling, perched a small black beret; a tight scar sketched over a blade-thin nose, a rash of silver Romany rings, all shapes, on blushing fingers.

Watching the man, the way no one paid him any mind, the alone-ness of him in a pub where noise was important; the few true Irish who came in pretending to be IRA men on the run or some-such and the noise varnished the pretence, everyone working a fix, on the make, money-under-the-table men, papers-how-are-ye, a corrupt country spreading its corruption in man-sized molecules, the French barmen so utterly quiet and tolerant and ashamed of what they had to work with: he'd watched the man and discovered a kind of uneasy reflection and so the next time he came in *he* offered *him* a drink, watching the wet bluegrey eyes in the white plate face grapple with a mote of suspicion then open like a child's. He bought the man the drink as much as to say *I'm not like the rest in here, fakers and cowards, well I could define that if I wanted to, but you know what I mean, not real, the sorts of Irish that make you want to puke and spend half their lives puking, I came here to get away from them, what did you come here to get away from?*

He told the man over six or seven drinks that he hated his country and if that was too abstract, and everyone thought hatred of one's country was abstract, not enough in itself to make you do anything, he said it was politically corrupt and the man *humphed* and said *So is France* and he replied, feeling a tad disappointed that no, he didn't mean quite like that. He meant that the very air was corrupt; politics, the Arts, one was not a balance to the other, it came out of bog-poverty and generations of cheating the foreign landlord some said but that was Okay for Sunday newspaper columnists on fat wages to say, but it was more than that; the other man saying that in the Polish ghetto, *now I know you won't believe this*, the most *corrupt*, I mean morally corrupt, you know, the most *exploitative* of the ghetto Jews were other Jews, you're telling me nothing new, it is the history of people who don't know who they are anymore. Or who've let others tell them for too long.

He'd dribbled in a gaseous Martini, so delicate for working fingers, of travels by train and wearing tags and being smaller than the other children and yes, you might call me a Jew, but I lost the real part of that in London over the years, Anglicans, not church-goers, didn't say yes or no, just ignored I was a Jew, but they were the nicest people in the world, dead now, I learned to call them my family, they reared me, a snotty child with a name-tag round his neck, they had none of their own, get me? My own, don't ask, I never bothered. Smoke, most like. And before you say it, why does the *Yid* always start defining history from *Those Days?* Because for some of us, I suppose, there was nothing before that matters and less afterwards, in terms of *who we really are*, especially the children, like me, but I don't really give a fuck. Cheers.

More to it than that, I know what I mean but it's hard to define, he'd argued, Ireland has nothing to compare, I hadn't thought where you started your history from, but I had imagined The King David Hotel would be an equally defining place; and the look, sad as a robbed child, in the man's marine-glossy eye, as if he'd found a friend and lost one in the same moment, or hadn't said the right thing, or had been crudely misinterpreted; music just starting, the *diddle-eye* in the background, got him on to the subject of what the Church had done in Ireland to little children. What drink does to you, he heard himself say none too gracefully, to the man; I apologise, I am not anti-Jewish. I don't know where that came from. From history, the man said, you're obviously a *history* man. *Don't apologise.* Anyway, it had nothing to do with me. My Jerusalem is *here,* and *this* – banging the bar-top – is my Wailing Fucking Wall.

Why did you call yourself a Yid, it's not a nice name?

What's in a name? *Fuck* you, Paddy. The Irish are the most racist people in the world, especially when they're not at home. We're a poor second, particularly when we're not real. *Drink up.*

At that stage in drink when nothing's an insult. Or when murder can happen over a silly remark. No one knowing quite who he is any longer, or what side's up. Rings catching the squalid light. A *Planxty* poster, years old, on a wall.

The guard whistled a tune. It sounded like Jazz. There was such good, such young Jazz, in and around Paris and the best place was over on the Left, which wasn't what it had been but still had the *caveaux* and *caves* here and there where the young bucks tried their hands. All the Black great Jazzmen who'd played Paris. *History.* And the guard whistling the tune reminded him that the painter had taken him there to meet her one evening, the very first time, and after that had come the studio and the end of his known life.

The *avocat* came under the scaffolded shadow of the Tour St. Jacques; a fat cripple's leg in splints. Few in Paris, he mused, could remember when the remains of the church had been free of its callipers. He walked on, enjoying the rue de Rivoli in its lunchtime, men as well-suited as himself carrying baguettes filled with cheese, sausage, ham, God knows what, eating contentedly as they walked. Young women chattering, dragging flags of perfume behind them, in bird-like clusters, walking as if there were an emergency in the air.

In his slim, professional briefcase he carried, among his papers, a dog-eared paperback of a novel by Gabriel Chevallier, like him, a native of Lyon – and unlike him, a bearer of the Croix de Guerre and a Chevalier de la Legion d'Honneur. A talented hero; an enviable thing. Not *un plouc,* a hick. A skin to rub off, discard; a pupa to shed. To prove himself, then, in the big city, Piaf's *Paname*. Anyway......

There were sales in some of the shops, brash 'Soldes' signs taped across the windows; a good pair of dressy, but casual, shoes wouldn't go amiss. But he gave himself no time to stop. As if he were two people, the one who wished to window-crawl for shoes, and the other who pressed on to some urgent assignation.

It was, as always, a longer walk than he had anticipated; the Métro had been crowded, airless, intimidating, but he'd allowed for that. He'd even given up his flappable door-seat to an elderly Moroccan woman, her face heavily stamped and decorated in blue ink. Such things made you feel decent.

At first, as always, he couldn't see Marcel. There was that half-second of a speeded-up heart, an anxiety he detested. The little square sloped gently towards the rue de Rivoli, a restaurant on either side. Wicker chairs and chairs of steel tubing rested, occupied and precarious, beside circular, busy tables. There was a subtle, eager noise from inside Marcel's restaurant. Not *Marcel's*, really. Just where he worked. Gone the professional waiters in their aprons and black waistcoats; Marcel appeared in tight faded jeans, a yellow top with the face of George W. Bush printed on it; Bush wore a cowboy hat and his body was very small, and very small hands fired tiny pistols in every direction.

Marcel was thin, tall, his head and face shaven. He had nut-brown eyes and his skin too was delicately browned. His Semitic nose gave away his half-Algerian parentage. With great deftness, he balanced a round tin tray in one hand, and on the tray sat two plates of assorted salad and a woven yellow basket of bread. The *avocat's* breathing slowed down, but he couldn't ignore the tightness in his throat. Marcel was beautiful. He was a lucky man.

"'jour, petit!"

Marcel, not unbalancing the tray by a degree, leaned over and kissed him on the cheek. The tables were crowded, there was nowhere to sit. Marcel bounced off, came back with the tray dragging down by his side.

"I bought you decent shoes. You wear *these.*"

Marcel pulled a clown's face. An angel trying to look like a devil.

"For here, they are comfortable. I would destroy good shoes. I love you for your decent shoes."

"Oh, stop. Find me a place."

"Anything for you."

"Stop, I'm hungry!"

Someone shouted something at Marcel, from the dimmer distances of the restaurant's interior. Marcel cocked his ass. The *avocat* didn't really like it when it all got so.... what was the word?

A couple of businesswomen got up from a small round table, an explosion, like ducks from cover, of colours and flapping and hurried noises. Marcel rushed upon them, hands to the bill, the money, the tip, hoisted their used plates and cutlery on to his tray, made a showy brushing down of a chair.

"For *Maître l'avocat.*"

"Are you joining me."

"I will. Five minutes. Maybe two, that's all. How was your day?"

Marcel seated himself on the edge of a chair across the table. Traffic on the rue de Rivoli honked and banged and blared and on their little square, someone started up a big Japanese motorbike. You couldn't hear anything else but the background noise. Then it was gone, a blue petrolly smoke in the air, and they looked at each other.

"My day was the prison again."

Marcel's cool fingers were on his wrist now, his snow-white shirt cuff a few centimetres from those manicured nails. Marcel was the most fastidious man he'd ever met. He changed his socks twice a day, maybe three times. But now and then, his dress sense, a childish defiance.....

"My poor boy."

"I hate that place. Every time I have to go there, I feel I leave something of myself behind."

Marcel said nothing. A good listener.

"I shouldn't bring this to you."

"Who else should you bring it to? I love you."

For a moment he could only smile. Marcel made everything simple, stripped away the complications, said *This is how things are.* As a teenager, he'd had petrol poured over him up in the towers of la Cité because the others found out he was queer, and only emergency surgery had saved him from being a eunuch. As it was, the scars, red, thick, mapped out the bottom of his belly and thighs as if mapping the Atlas Mountains.

"What will you eat?"

He eyed the menu. Perhaps he didn't really want to talk.

"Omelette. *This* one. Frites, I suppose. No salad. A glass of white."

Marcel scribbled quickly. He could work in a court, he should be a reporter.

"I've news too," said Marcel. "Not much, but to me, a lot. Two poems. In *La Mouette.*"

"What do you mean, 'Not much'? I think that's terrific! When?"

"September, perhaps. You know how they are. Takes so long, the feeling of accomplishment vanishes by the time you get the magazine."

"I've seen a copy of *La Mouette* on someone's desk in my office. It's widely read."

Marcel moved back a step.

"You're a liar. But that's Okay. A liar in a good cause."

He couldn't help but laugh. Marcel kissed him again on the cheek and walked away, a man's walk, muscular, nothing mincing there. He'd played football once. Some said he'd been not at all bad. Now he wrote and worked at the restaurant. Or worked at the restaurant and wrote.

Three years is a long time, the *avocat* thought happily. Life has been good to us.

Once inside the restaurant, Marcel shouted and bantered with the rest. My father, thought the *avocat*, would've walked straight out of any restaurant that didn't have professional, aproned waiters. He opened his briefcase, looking for his novel.

But the first thing that fell out was his mini-cassette recorder. As it struck the ground it started up, and for a few seconds, until he claimed it again and shut it off, it emitted the voice of his Irish client. From under the table, the voice sounded like an insect scraping against a piece of tin.

Confident enough with what money he'd given her and what she'd stolen, the girl is in no hurry, took the Métro to Parmentier; and there, rising into the hot, yelling air of that spoked wheel of Paris, one of many, she's thrown herself down with studied carelessness at a wickered table outside the café, *Le Parmentier*, seated herself under the great neon letters, ordered coffee from a gentlemanly waiter almost as old as the painter and in full aproned garb, the men in the bar bitching about horse-racing, poring over racing-pages, spitting and smoking.

A lazy Alsatian brooded in the sawdust. Heads came up, then full bodies, materialising out of the Métro station straight-backed and strangely stiff, like characters in a zombie movie she'd once seen rising out of the earth. All around her the great cliffs of Hausmann's city reared up; how tidily people kept their balconies, their windows! How prettily!

It seemed to her that every balcony possessed a window-box and every window-box was full to the brim with flowers of every imaginable colour. In the grey heights, these tender explosions of colour. Here and there a woman leaned

15

out and cropped this and watered that, you could see over their heads the high ornate ceilings, the pictures on the walls. On the rooftops, the impossibly high windows of attic rooms, expensive, with views over the roofs of Paris as far as Montmartre, or anywhere else, for that matter. At the level of the street, there were great spilling palettes of colour where the fruit and vegetable stalls were; oranges, bananas, melons split open, apples, lemons, limes, courgettes, potatoes, tomatoes, lettuces, fat onions, scallions, strings of silvery garlic, peas in slim green pods, kidney beans in pale yellows and deep red – she could not make out every shape, but she could see the colours. Dark small men moved in and out of the Arab shops, it didn't matter that Turks owned so many of them, that's what they were called because they'd open late at night and on weekends, the shops that sold everything from henna for your hair to lightbulbs to bottles of Scotch to cornflakes; they smiled at each other, welcomed friends with their fingers lightly touching their breasts, the kisses on each side of the face, the long robes dangling over the hot dust of the street. A carpet-seller, hefting his wares across one shoulder, was stopped suddenly by a stranger and there in the middle of the unnoticing street a haggle began, a passionate mime; the carpet-seller would walk away, shaking his head, then he'd come back; this time it was the stranger's turn to walk away, return. Choreography, wonderful to look at, that ended in a handover of notes and a small carpet. Now two men walked away from each other, each with something bobbing up and down on his shoulders.

With her coffee came a wrapped square of mint chocolate. She opened it carefully, as if she might never do such a thing again. The painter had bought her a coffee just like this one, piled with cream, hot, sweet, frothy, in a wide cup, with a square of wrapped chocolate too, when he'd first met her, when she'd indicated that he could fuck her for the coffee and he'd refused. And she'd tried her luck, as you could always do with lonely men, especially the older ones who saw you as a daughter first and a whore second, who fought with this ambiguity while you played with it; he'd bought her soup, lots of bread came with it, and then he'd bought her a glass of red wine. She wasn't used to drinking wine from a glass, or couldn't recall when she'd last done so. At any rate something in the way she drank from the glass made the painter smile under his mad red banner of dyed hair. *You are a nymph in something by Cimabue. Or Clodion, before the Revolution buggered him up.* She'd watched his lips chewing articulate, used French, with a realistic semblance of the street. *You haven't a clue what I'm talking about, have you?* With the lightest touch, he stroked her hair, just once. She could smell thinners on his fingers. With a lot of the truckers, it was engine-oil or beer or semen. He bought her cigarettes, walked with his arm around her, and in one of those eternal corner-shops, ignoring the silences and the looks under the framed verses from the Koran and the pictures of Mecca, he'd bought a couple of bottles of wine, and eggs and bread for her breakfast.

At no point had he asked her to come home with him. It had happened, simply and without explanations, and she had found herself walking with him, wondering what to do next, because he did not want her to do what she normally did. And he did not seem to mind in the least that she stared at his lips to know what he said because she was deaf, or that she made signs with her hands or just pointed to make herself understood, because she was mute. She'd learned that men didn't mind that, didn't mind that you didn't understand them and couldn't speak to them. It was enough to open your legs. Then they made that weird, pained face, then were ashamed of you, they paid you, walked away hating you. Or tried, as one had, to strangle you.

You're a child. Are you even eighteen? Oh, what am I doing with you! Are you on drugs?

They'd reached the flagstoned yard. He'd fiddled with keys, muted clack of keys against rings. He didn't seem to require any kind of response.

Welcome to my Cour des Miracles!

She wondered, briefly, if he might be mad. If he might murder her.

Down the street was a fire-station, and all of a sudden the great gates rose and there was a flash of steel and a flickering of hysterical lights and a sudden shift in the tides of traffic around her. The great engines, two of them, barged their way up the street, shoving smaller vehicles aside. When they were gone, the air seemed to settle. She sucked the sugary froth from the bottom of her ample cup. She wiped chocolate from her mouth.

She'd needed something. Then she'd run away, then she'd returned, exhausted, physically sick and paranoid, her head a brothel of banlieusards' double-speak, their weird and magical *verlan*. She suspected that her *revendeuse*, a nymph not much older than herself, cheated her, speaking in that back-to-front slang so that she couldn't read her lips properly. In any case, she wrote him a ragged note in which she said she didn't use needles. He asked her to stay with him. She slept and shook for two days.

All she stood up in, even the neat cut of her hair, she owed to him.

There was always someone singing at the end, or perhaps the beginning, of the corridor, and he could almost make out the words; he'd heard it before, something crazy, Johnny Hallyday when he was still trying to be Elvis. How long had he been here that he knew things like that, the phases a French pop singer went through? Were bits of history, culture, slips of life picked up by a kind of osmosis? Was simply being here enough?

The time to really be here was the 'Sixties. It was all happening then. Algerians tossed into the Seine, students rioting in the streets, factories on strike, the muscular tang of tear-gas. He'd come too late, if he was looking for that sort of tension in the air, well, you wouldn't get it back home, everything flat, dead, no one moving, even the great demos against Bush flying his death-planes into Shannon Airport seemed like a mime of something else, something greater that never happened, and could never happen, you lived with that. The 'planes came; Paddy was a clown, the factories closed down anyway; old pubs with old songs and old men singing them, coughing their lungs out and pissing in their pants.

He was in a balloon, floating over Paris, not touching down in any of it; the Judas-hole clicked open, a black place for an instant where the guard's eye was, all's well, he wasn't hanging from the ceiling. Last night they'd dragged in a couple of Irish drunks, singing, for an instant he'd been tempted to shout down *Here! Over here! I'm with you!* Which was not patriotism or solidarity but a primal reflex, embarrassing, really; and then he'd heard them yell and the soft *whish* of something been squirted and one of them screaming *I'm blind! I'm blind!* And the grubby cackle of a guard laughing. *That* scared you, no mistake *there, 'sieur!* They were quiet boys after that! *Hup, ya boy-yah!* Dump you in the Seine quick as look at you, but he had to admire something about them all the same, something he wasn't, a *knowing who they were* that you didn't see back home, where everything came from somewhere else or belonged to someone else. What the painter had said, revealing himself as a painter down in the basement of the Jazz club, *Caveau Mouche,* under Paris, right under the skin of the city, while the place filled up with young people, anyone in the world was younger than him now, and a four-piece got itself together, upright piano, drums, double-bass, sax, the curved dripping room taking off in the smoke and beer, the young French couples didn't drink enough to drown a mouse; what he'd said about the way a Frenchman, however bad, could point to the best in the Musée d'Orsay and say *That came out of us, that changed the world of seeing forever,* even the pioneers of film had a name that reflected light: *Lumière,* it was all too much to take in, the Irish had given the world the man who said *The only good Injun's a dead Injun* and a Catholic President who fucked cheerleaders like an Olympic athlete taking hurdles. A twinge of defiance, of hurt, when he'd said that? Maybe so, but that was natural.

The way the young beardless Jazz players had it organised was that every now and then they'd stop playing, fiddle about with their sheets of music, mutter to each other like priests at a rite, then they'd announce to the hushed and huddled room that they were going to play So-and-So and they needed, no offence, a horn man who knew it; then he'd noticed, slipped by him somehow, that blokes had arrived carrying weird-shaped cases, they'd congregated near the stage or what passed for a stage, waiting their chance and sure enough, someone would step up, grunting his name, opening his case at the same time, take out the required instrument, sometimes a horn, sometimes anything short of a drum-kit or an upright and even then sometimes a stranger would take over, sit at the keys, get behind the top-hat, test it with a tinny tap; there was cheering and the tune kicked off, each instrument feeling its way in slowly, like a man making love to a new woman for the first time, not wishing to hurt, or embarrass, to disturb; finding the depth of the tune, working in and out and around it, the new player on stage getting his grip, riding the tune until he could find his own pace, not theirs, then taking off and doing his own thing and getting his applause. No more than two tunes to any new guy, and the place, in a couple of hours, was blazing with sweat, smoke, beer, music, heat, youth. He couldn't *ever* leave. He just wished he could play an instrument. Maybe the paint-headed half-Yid painter with the neon-red hair and a mistake of a thread of red trickly beard on a face like a bruised polished plate would feel him up at the end of the night, he'd be ready for that if that's what was going to happen and he'd break his neck, but you had to be thankful to be brought here, just to feel the music for a half-second, to be out of your own skin and floating halfway up the saxophone, whatever he had been or had come from less than a blot on a piece of toilet-

20

paper blowing along the ratty gutters outside in the street, getting caught and dampened out of existence against the sodden wrapped sacks jammed into the drain mouths to stop the river dissolving Lutetia back into her Roman swamp.

Then she'd come in, the girl the painter had or had not mentioned, a little nervous thing, just a teenager and only just, and she'd seen him and smiled, a jacket over her shoulder made of some shiny plastic silver material, and a tight crotch-deep pair of jeans and the painter had said into his hot brass-deafened little ear: *This is the woman I love.*

With time to kill, he had too much time. He found himself staring into the window of an antique musical instruments' shop somewhere off the Place des Vosges, how he'd walked all the way up there he had no idea. The heat, which rose up from the pavement, from every wall and window, down out of the defiantly blue sky, dragged his jacket off him, rolled up his sleeves and jammed a plastic bottle of Evian into his hand, the contents of which warmed up with the swelter of his own skin. Every human being who passed him by drew after them his or her own particular draught of heat, uniquely perfumed, as if the sun was drawing a layer of personality from everyone, much as a surgeon performing an autopsy might lightly peel the skin back from a skull.

The *avocat* stared through his reflection in the glass, into a world of flashing, brassy wonders. Ancient fat-bellied mandolins hung from pegs on the dark – therefore, perhaps, cool – lunch-shut interior.

Here a small and curious guitar, stringless; an enormous tarnished tuba backed by a fifedom of abrupt wooden flutes; violins, one of which bore on its back a delightful scene of Versailles with coiffured women dancing against a sloping garden, languished on perilous strings from unseen hooklets in the ceiling close to the big window. An ancient piano, thin and with its mouth of broken keys like a drunkard's teeth, hid unplayable under an enormous and old poster advertising a performance of something illegible by Puccini; an instrument more curious than any, a sort of piano where the stringboard was perpendicular, standing up like a vainglorious harp, occupied a bright spot in the shadows at the back of the room; and there too, visible, was the proprietor's desk, a *portable* recharging on its stand, a stack of fliers of all sorts falling over the desk. Sheets of music, some wrapped in red string and others resting between crumbling covers, lay in heaps all over the floor beneath the window; a venerable accordion, its bellows shattered, rested sadly under the silvery proud name of 'Vestaglione,' while down the very back wall slithered a *serpente*, a winding wood-and-brass wind instrument that seemed, as he looked at it, to move. He drew back the focal point of his eyes and stared at his reflection in the window, then through his reflection into the room, and wondered whether a million tiny reflections of himself lay unmoving and vigilant in the polished backs of violins, the rumps of trombones, along the languid slides of trombones, and images smaller still, on the foggy silvery keys of flutes; and he recalled the famous black and white photograph by François Seignard of a man carefully photographing his reflection in a window photographing his reflection in a window photographing his reflection in a win.... and on and on into a mind-wrenching infinity of images. In his content state of mind, and with his belly full, the *avocat* gave himself over to musings on arcane and mesmerising theories....

"Now, I never knew you played, Hervé."

He turned spastically, shocked out of his quiet philosophical speculations, the water in his plastic bottle sloshing distantly. Before him stood a very thin young man in a designer pair of summer slacks, silky and shiny, an open-neck pure white silk Charvet and light but expensive leather shoes. His short black hair was tossed about with great care and jelled. He looked like a successful footballer; he had Marcel's semi-dark features, but his nose was small and suburban. On his wrist glistered a remarkable Swiss watch. An expensive scent issued from him like a decree. His clean-shaven face gleamed. He appeared not to sweat.

The *avocat* recognised a notary who, as was whispered at any rate, narrowly lost the vote to become one of the youngest of his trade ever to sit on the bench of the Conseil Supérieur du Notariat. A young man swiftly on the up.

"I don't, I'm afraid."

Instinctively, he moved away from the shop window. He felt some sad daydream dissolve in the air behind them as they walked. The street sloped upwards, there were cafés and a distant *tabac* and a small guardian army of black-painted iron posts, waist-high, all the way along the pavement. Here and there, appearing suddenly beside them, was a take-away or eat-in Turkish kebab shop, the noise of Turkish singing and the spicy burning meat smells, not to mention the carpets of door-heat suddenly flung in your face, the last straw on such a deadly afternoon. The fat-armed men behind the counters with their dark moustaches seemed to look at your contemptuously. Weary garnishes of salad leaves and deflated tomatoes lay in moist white trays.

"Day off," the *avocat* lied.

The thought of conversation was too much. He wanted very much for this young man to go away. In the Napoleonic corridors, down the wide Sun King allies and stairs, some with oddly telling names – the Merchant's Corridor, for example – where light was cold as stone no matter what it was like outside and everything echoed into acute and thick-doored distances, the *avocat* plied his trade, while this young man, making better money, crabbed the small delicate estates of widows and the futures of newlyweds and purchasers of strips of land or brick like a character from Balzac or Flaubert. And then the *avocat* had a troubling thought, a flash of something from years ago. But the young man strolling by his side had begun to speak.

"I hear this Irishman of yours is a loser. A loser for *you,* that is. And possibly the Irish will complain. French police brutality's always a good one, notions too of foreign law being somehow denying of human rights because the framework's different, and so on. You'll have to travel to Dublin, almost certainly...."

"I can't discuss it. You understand."

They walked on a little further. The silence was oppressive. At last he could take it no more and he stopped. He looked the young man in the eye, angry not at him but at a memory. The young *notaire* would become rich on wedding agreements, inheritances and contracts of sale; he would never sit across a filthy metal table in a locked cell and talk to murderers. The young man smelled of money and good family and privilege – the *avocat* was suddenly powerless against a hot tide of old prejudices.

"I am on my lunch-break. Go find yourself a rich widow who can't read a will."

The young man began to object; that is, he raised slowly his expensively-timepieced arm.

"I do not wish to appear rude, but please fuck off," said the *avocat*, ashamed of himself even as he spoke.

"That's no way....."

"And another thing. You and I are *not* on first name terms, *M'sieur.* I am sorry but that's the way it is. How many times have we greeted each other – two, three? I have to go."

The young man's face had reddened and, like a suspect suddenly caught out in a lie, he was gearing himself up for argument. Right there in the street. In front of the Turks with the big hairy arms and their way of looking at you. But the *avocat* had already moved on. The two men looked like lovers who'd had a tiff, one standing, the other walking. A guttural phrase at the counter of the closest kebab house and a gust of lusty laughter from somewhere in the back; the young man straightened himself and disappeared.

He loathed himself. He wanted to strip out of this old, angry skin – was his anger visible? Did it have a smell? – and become new even in the flesh. And as he strode farther and farther up the gentle incline of the street, the *avocat*, feeling the tug of the loop in his jacket squeeze harder on his index finger as he dangled it over his shoulder, felt a blush of sun on his neck. At university he had been merely another redneck from the depths of a country the Paris boys knew little of and cared less about, even those who pondered a life in politics. The air was still heady with the essence of '68, *les événements* – somebody'd dragged a piano into a Sorbonne hall, there was singing around it, *Nous sommes chez nous!* loud in the air, *It is forbidden to forbid!* Cohn-Bendit poised like a bird behind the microphones, a thin, anxious bird, Danny-the-Red, the Banque de France on strike, de Gaulle on the radio, the heft of a paving-block in your hand, the CRS looking like an army of invented robots, the smoke – though by now too many of those barrier heroes, each one a *fils-de-papa*, is a lecturer in an English tweed jacket – an aftertaste that was bitter with disappointment and not a little spicy rage at having been just that little bit too late. He and some others had come together to form their own society, a sweet and occasionally challenging guild of some dozen members, men and women, who couldn't stand the gentle but serious ribbing every day; they were hicks, sons and daughters of pig-farmers and, those who were Breton were known to fuck their brothers and sisters. They had a young Algerian fellow student who, ostracised for other reasons, had been proposed by someone of a liberal cast of mind for membership but, well, you had to draw the line somewhere – he shivered now at that memory, the unctuous and transparently hypocritical blather in which the refusal had been couched. They called themselves *les flaubertois*, after the notions proposed by that failed Rouen lawyer in his *Madame Bovary*, adjusting playfully the novelist's angle on provinciality to suit their own purposes, proud under every irony and contradiction, but a label's better than no label. Behind their enthusiasm and bonded defiance, he knew from his own experience that there lurked a black and viperish envy, call it an anger, to be honest.

Anyone who has to form a special society around him in order to confront the world has already been beaten by it.

Les flaubertois may have had its mocking, joking side; but its very existence marked its members even more thoroughly as provincials and outsiders doing some intellectual rummaging in a Paris university like tramps in a flea-market. After a time it disbanded, its members fleeing, like him, into what Parisian professions would have them; the Algerians served the Algerians, the Bretons worked best among the music-mad cider-lampers in the restaurants and cafés where cholesterol-thick cakes sweetened the urge for civil litigation. One dead Sunday he took a train to Rouen, to the planet that had given birth to *les flaubertois*, took a look up at the rain-drenched and rust-scaffolded front of the cathedral and skulked back to Paris, having a drunken snooze on the upstairs of the train.

For some reason the young *notaire* and the heat, the Swiss watch, the light leather shoes, the odour of expense, his being whipped out of his reverie, had thrown up memories of loneliness and isolation, of being young and melancholy in an enormous and unnavigable city, and he had taken it out on the young man, which was unforgivable, when all was said and done, maybe he was only trying to be civil. Perhaps he would seek him out, apologise. He particularly couldn't thank him for that recollection of how *les flaubertois* all treated the Algerian, not letting him join, cogging whispery arguments why not, feeling themselves distinctly superior to him just as they felt inferior to everyone else.

And most definitely he should have known better, that frivolous young man, not to get so damned familiar and not to ask questions about his case. But telling him to fuck off, using language like that, was not good, the incident could end up in the wrong ears.

He was exhausted now. He could walk no further. His vital notes were in his desk or on his desk and his desk seemed so far away, on the other side of the world. He had work to do. He felt fretful and anxious. He crossed the street and hailed a taxi. Then he scurried all the way back down to the rue St Antoine and on an island in the middle of the street he joined a queue of people hotly screaming at passing taxis. He was mad with impatience now.

When at last one drew alongside, he pushed a young woman out of the way and, to the outraged sound of her accusations and swearing, shut the back door of the taxi and gave the night-black North African driver directions.

He was able to sleep, dollops of drowsing. He would hear the click of the Judas being opened and the quickening of his heart each time. But he had begun to refuse to open his eyes, an act of defiance, yes, something silly like that, but what there was to hold on to; here he was, then, and the walls of the cell had stopped moving in and out, pulsating like lungs filling and emptying with the warm cigarette anxiety of prisoners like himself, he could hear them in spasms of shuffling sound, or in a shout, or a rattle or screech of a door opening; there were sounds from the streets, however far away beyond his cell he could only imagine, cars revving up, horns going, a hush of trees, a woman's shout; it was bizarre, unreal, as if someone had decided to lock him away from these normal things as some kind of joke. The painter had told him you hate your country because it is your father you really hate and that had seemed to make an awkward kind of sense at the time, working his way around his studio, that dark, one-window-lighted place whose light was always very old, as if it had rested, trapped in a courtyard, for centuries, something fatherly and repulsive about his red clownish shag of hair, his whitewashed, red-framed face that seemed, though it couldn't be true, never to have seen the sun, the nose-scar sometimes blooming like a flower; and sometimes, for no reason that seemed obvious, the painter, hunched, would give off an odour of cheap aftershave, some *après-rasage* grabbed out of the bright mouth of an Arab shop

27

and paid for in his London French, the red etch of beard ragged; the room he worked in was a gloomed clutter of decaying things, old furniture, paintings stacked against and on top of each other, finished, unfinished, books on painting, painters, newspapers turning yellow with smoke and age and of course there was the constant smoke, the cigarettes, the Craven 'A' which he had never seen before and which the painter sucked on night and day, one after the other, so that even with the small window opened the room was a chemical catastrophe of smells of burning tobacco and thinners. The paintings seemed to have glued their style to a stiff, elderly intensity, visually fantastic; people, the painter said, had gone back to a more *concrete* manner because the rubbish that went about posing as art these days, well, the colleges no longer taught drawing skills and that said it all; but he suspected that the painter had flung himself deliberately for God only knew what vague reason back to a stylistic period in cultural history which he believed *morally* superior to our own; that there was something morally – for the painter at any rate – more acceptable about the style and culture of an earlier time, though he had often wondered how, as a Jew or half-Jew, the painter could ever have placed his trust in history. He was in ways like a man who, hearing stories from his parents of a homeland he has never known, longs gradually not merely to go there for the first time in his life, but to *return* there. So he makes it up. It was possible always to look into the painter's portraits, past those very modern faces and those *haute-couture* smiles, and see a modern Paris suburb staring out from a Parthenon hill.

He saw, and understood, that it would be virtually impossible to reconstruct with any oath-weighted accuracy so much as one hour of a day spent mooching about without money in that studio, then sleeping on the destroyed couch while the painter took the girl off, or she toddled after him, everyone nicely drunk on Arab-shop wine; and up the stairs the girl and the painter would go out of the contained quiet of the courtyard, its stone walls stained with old ivy. Had they talked, discussed things, and what sort of things? And he'd listen some nights until the painter whippled in orgasm and then a crushing silence fell over the courtyard, the street and the entire city of Paris, a silence like no other imaginable. Or to tell them what it was like to watch the oblong of yellow light find its place on the wall in front of him, half on and half off a portrait of some man or woman who had not paid, had not collected, had disappeared into the Parisian – or Attic, if you will – vastnesses like a thought dissolving; then you would see half a painting, like having half a dream, incomplete images sawn in half by light and how you, drunk nicely, thought of a past which did not exist save in half-snatches of remembering; a demonstration here, a march there, hands working on the construction of a banner which would be so full of wind when held aloft it weighed too much for its bearers, all this in the name of some otherwise inexpressible anger, something beyond politics, though few would admit it, something personal and beyond resolve, and somehow it came in, flurries of it like snow and feeble hail on a sunny day and wafted about that dark room, even as a scrabble of rat-sounds in the courtyard made him aware of his own present vulnerability, a bite could finish him off, he could die by some other method, by some atrocious accident, here in a foreign city and no one'd know, he'd written hasty postcards in spasms.

So it was always in a vague fog of anxiety, drunk or sober, that he drifted off to sleep, what sleep was possible in a bombed couch in such a room of staring painted faces and squeak and scratch sounds, which may have been the pages of old magazines shifting or some plague heading his way on sharp yellow teeth; and how in God's name to explain to them the tear he'd feel in his gut or somewhere to hear the painter's anguished cry of pleasure, the girl never made anything like that, she could make no sound at all.

They'd taken his watch, as if robbing him of time itself, and he had no idea what time it was or what portion of the day.

The young lawyer had come to him how many times now? The meetings with the Irish civil servant, though, were the most harrowing of all: the grey country face, the mountainy farmer's face looking at him above a tight white shirt and a strangling blue tie, a shirt that had decided to do its wearer damage; the embarrassed, or was it annoyed?, look of the man, broken by late middle-age: *A mess, this, you know, and the French jurisdiction. With the complicated way they handle the law.* This farmer or farmer's son would shake his head, rummage in a brown leather satchel. *And you without a penny, it won't go down well.* He'd had money but he'd given it to the girl, everything he had, so insane had those last hours been, the knowledge that he could own nothing in the world and would have been better, like the painter, stepping into a world which may or may not have existed but whose stark bones you could flesh out any way you wished for as long as you wished and even put part of the real world in it if you liked. He'd mentioned a prominent political party back home, just its name, and the puffing, searching Irishman had stopped what he was doing and looked at him. *Meaning what, the situation you're in! We know all about you.* Leaving it there, hanging, rummaging again for things that could never be found, annoyed, a man out of his depth; the photographers on rooftops, the helicopter that always seemed to play the coveting angel over every demo, every march to the airports, every protest on every street in Ireland.

And how to explain to anyone how all of it, now, in this cell, seemed like a play that had just finished, curtain down, sets pushed away, to reveal the bare walls of the stage, this cell, upon which the only actors were shadows cast by his own body and directed by the single wired-up bulb in the high ceiling and a shadow of light from a high, barred window?

Fortified by coffee, by the gregarious movement of traffic and people, she moved without hurry along a street that sloped downwards, every street from here pouring itself into the

Seine, past fruit-stalls like palette-spills of paint, launderettes full of revolving movement, almost like dance, and African women, robed in blues, browns, yellows and talking high above the machines; past Arab displays of mats, carpets, scarves, wooden flutes, boxes of henna with smiling young women on them – their faces uncovered, that wouldn't do! – everything hanging in this window or from that door, men in shadow talking loudly, dark faces lined, etched, carved; a great rambunction of activity, movement, impression; downhill, down, like walking in a carnival that never seemed to end, that was pulled downwards as if laid out on an enormous children's slide; and then a window would open, or one half of those massive wooden doors with lion's heads doorknobs, on the wall next to it a marble square with a date, a name, and *Mort pour la patrie* stamped on it in fading gold lettering, and a beautiful young man would scamper out, jump on his pushbike with rehearsed abandon, and she'd watch him, how the curves of his body fitted the machine, how the lines of his arms rippled as he began to steady it; then he'd be gone, disappeared into the heart of the traffic, the movement; her foot kicked a discarded plastic Yop container, it toc-tocked hollowly beyond her ears into the gutter where a bright silver snake of water slid along with the tiniest of trickles and the container shook for a moment and moved off clumsily, carried on the weak flow.

She thought too often for her own good of that first moment, when, seeing him in the basement Jazz club she'd been awakened as a light bulb is turned on to a possibility of other, though remote, things; and how, with the painter rising to wave her over, that possibility or whatever it had been evaporated or was expunged as if it had run out of breath. Moving her slim body – she was proud of how slim it was, how relatively undamaged – among the tables, watching with eyes that were not on the front of her head how young men inspected her, the hollow uncertain dip between her legs which was eye-level with them, how this was where men always looked, even in the street, she found her head filling up with unwanted, certainly undesirable, images of the painter touching her for the first time, how those images had arisen she didn't know, and how she had gone to him, a lonely man doing good things for her, out of kindness, as a mother gives milk to a child. How solemn, almost sad, he had been that first time, his French disappearing altogether, lipping things, gentle sweet things, which she could not translate but whose mouthed shapes she made out perfectly. How it had become different slowly, for no reason she could think of, how he had made love to her as if he detested the sight of her, that was the way it was these days, and more besides.

And here was this young man, no teenager, but younger, who smiled to see her, politeness, stood up though there wasn't room to stand up, and stayed on his feet while she found a chair and then offered drinks all round. She was amused and delighted, dare she think *flattered*, by the young man's surprise when he watched her muteness and deafness take shape in front of him, at least she was that much of a mystery to him, though some men were put off by deaf-mute girls because they carried the imagined, or superstitious – *Years ago, I'd be burned as a witch* – taint of something damaged and incurable about them, the contagion of silence; the painter leaned over, had the audacity to tip his mouth and one ear with a nicotine-painted finger, she could have slapped him in the face for that, let the stranger have his mystery. The painter kissed her, this cheek, then this one, and introduced her to the young man with the spiky enthusiasm she had come to associate with his having had too much to drink. If he beat her tonight, she'd leave. It was a mantra she recited to herself and she had faith in it, as one might have faith in a god one cannot see.

The young man coming back, fighting his way, angling his way – she watched the curves and movements of *his* body now – with a bottle or two, she chose beer, and now the musicians frantic and frayed, drifting as too much experimenting made them do, and the painter leaned over, not really caring whether she could see his lips and in any case she couldn't understand the shapes of his English: *I like all sorts of Jazz, but I do wish they'd give us a Boris Vian song. If you haven't heard Vian, then you haven't heard France, or a large part of it. They used to argue over authorship of his songs, he wrote so many of the fucking things.* She watched the fluid shapes the musicians made with their bodies, every part of their bodies, hands, faces, as they moved around their instruments, and imagined what the sounds made by such movements and gestures must be like; and it was as if the painter had stepped for an instant into another room, then come out again. On days when he, for no reason, was very happy, or his work was going well and she could do as she pleased, he played Vian with the *Quintet du Hot Club de France* and Django Reinhardt on the guitar, she read the sleeve notes on the CD which had a picture of Vian on the cover, smiling, nursing a revolver in his lap, she assumed by the little green light and the revolving disk and the empty CD case that Vian was playing; and there was one memorable day, even the neighbours pigeoned out of their windows, when he'd flung wide open the single window of the studio, turned a knob on his player and, grabbing her by the hand, dragged her into the hot, sunblasted courtyard and danced with her, swinging her here and there, her silent laughter coming unbidden from nowhere she could possibly imagine, no source she thought she possessed, *Da-dada, da-dada, da-dada-da-da,* he was out of breath, making these rhythmic shapes with his teeth, tongue and his mouth, his shirt flapping obscenely as his trousers made their way below his waist, and the women in the windows shouting and one of them clapping and lip-shaping happy vulgar things. She couldn't hear a word he said nor a note of Vian's music. And now for a moment the painter had dragged her into that sunny place with him again; then they were back in the smoky basement, the beer bottles making cold rings on the table, their cigarettes giving them that *noir* glamour, or so she imagined, she liked the Jazz basements for their atmosphere of vague furtiveness, or revolution, or crime. The painter's nose-scar sweated, his fortune-teller's rings blinked skittishly.

Out in the night again, the lights of the *bateaux-mouches* coldly thumbing the yellow walls of the river, sliding along them like tongues of white ice over the ribs of majestic buildings, how they'd cut a nice trio of friends, walking loosely, kicking the ground, laughing or smiling, it scarcely mattered which, the painter putting an arm around her shoulder declaiming drunkenly in his precise funny French into her face things like *You see over there? That's where I sold my first painting;* and you'd try to look at his lips needing the barest flick of an eye and then to where his hand pointed and there would be nothing but a solid and stately government building buttressing the road, no gallery, nothing remotely like a gallery, and you'd have to ask yourself what he was indicating and what he meant, and there was the corner restaurant blazing with light like a ship on fire where he made you sit down at a wicker table on a wicker seat and a sudden cool breeze came off the river unexpected and chilling then dissipated with a blown shapelessness from a newspaper riding by at the level of the pavement; inside, behind you, the noiseless glare and rattle of last drinks, last cigarettes, couples reluctant to face the night, the end of things. In the distance, over the rooftops, the rapid-eye blink of a blue police car light and down the river, if you stood out on the pavement, an answering wink from the pricking top of the *Tour Eiffel.*

And they'd crossed the boulevard Richard Lenoir, walked on without thinking of anything for a while, then stood for a moment watching fat men playing a last game of *boules* on an ancient sanded strip, the silver globes rolling and caressing, the concentration among the watching circle of men until the ball collided with another ball or missed, and then a breathy mouthing of swearing and praise, or the shapes of these things, rose up like a response at Mass, that tension, as if some small miracle were happening before their eyes, cigarettes falling out of their mouths, the sand under their feet laced with butts. There was a brief protectiveness here; when it was gone, when one or two of the men had noticed her, she moved away. Over her head, trees rooted in the bowels of the city swayed greenly and made her think for some reason of distant, lost, Sundays. In the protective round iron grilles at the bases of their trunks, cigarette packets, condom wrappers and odd bits of this and that lay imprisoned like a mendicant under the streets of Quasimodo's Paris.

Just as she had, the young man had become part of the studio, the courtyard, most likely without realising it was happening. An oasis. A haven. A net into which lost souls swam and struggled for a time before releasing themselves to a sort of unbreathing yet comforting paralysis. Being in the painter's bed was not the worst thing that could happen. On the second night of the young man's stay, she made signs to him that she wanted him to follow her. Shivering and anxious, she made some excuse to the painter, who fell sullen and stabbed at his canvas with a thick-haired brush. He *understood*. So she kissed him.

Then she was out through the gate, needing something again, something else, happily desperate, into Paris with this other man at her side, though she didn't need him or anyone.

He pissed loudly into the squat-down in the corner, the Arab toilet, and pulled on the chain that had no handle. The smell was ammoniac and rancid, he imagined disease, *rats in wet drains*, and backed away. Mindful of the sliding Judas in the door, closed his trousers, feeling ridiculously as if his mother were about to roll into the room and beat him. Then the cell descended into silence again and he felt the aloneness of far traffic and the endless metallic muttering of the prison. The heat in the cell was heavy as iron and not much lighter in the square exercise yard where he shuffled without enthusiasm over the packed earth, the others who were with him at that time of the day looking as cautious and hurt as he imagined he did. There was one, a bruiser, a street-kid, who went from one man to the next, watchful and sly as melting ice, offering rolled cigarettes of a bad quality and consenting to being refused custom with a shrug of his broad shoulders.

This man came towards him, walked boldly over to him in spite of a cursory shout from somewhere; the sun slanted a complete triangle down one side of the yard, whose brick walls were laced with barbed-wire and something else, and over them the sound of the city he'd come to be free in rushed up against the walls like waves against rocks, and this man, a smell coming off him of sweat and something animal, held out at a slope a handful of thin, ragged cigarettes and said something in a throaty, peeling accent; looking down at his shaved skull, noticing for the first time an enormous scab, brown and blue, on the very top of the man's head, a tumour of some sort, coarse around the edges like a satellite image of a small island in a sea of yellow, then the man's eyes catching him looking, feral eyes born watchful, he had not so much come from a womb as emerged from a burrow, and the man slapped him roughly on the side of his face for staring, for noticing. Again, and rougher, more authoritative, a shout from somewhere, perhaps Heaven itself, and the man waddled off, closing his mauling fist around the anorexic cigarettes, this was no way to behave, this was unexpected and terrifying, the man's blow was not so much painful as startling, like a Bishop's confirmation slap on the cheek, anointing you into something for life, which was both sacred and utterly useless, which demanded faith and surrender; he walked, as if nothing at all had happened, into the comparative triangular shade and another shout, then another, and he looked up and a guard, high up on the wall in a small steel room, beckoned to him to come out of the shade, into the light where – presumably – he could see him, let's not make more work than necessary; it was possible that the guard could turn his head and look into the city, into living streets, into the faces of people who went about their business without slapping one another. In that moment, feeling the heat resume its fingery rapping of the top of his head, he imagined that the cigarette seller's slap measured the difference between the jungle and civilisation, as the Bishop's slap measured the distance between salvation and damnation; things were that simple. A falling to the ground, the surface of the road, those others falling, stumbling, teetering, grabbing over him and all around him, a sudden scrum, a running nowhere just out of the way of the flailing police-batons, the blue shirts with no identity numbers on their shoulders, and the wire around the airport and some banners still visible even as he fell and the fat red sneaky water-cannon, though no one imagined with any seriousness that they'd be used on *our own*, yet the Alsatian dogs patrolled on leads the edges of the runway and when this had happened, when someone had sat down in the middle of the road and everyone had and the charge had begun, there was a moment, short and bitter, when he knew he had parted himself from himself, become a ghost in a pack of ghosts, or moved to some other place where extremely sudden and bad things happened and violence was always, always possible, a life as different from any lived by his friends..... and the fat US transport 'planes lay like grey winged maggots, nightmare things, on the tarmac runways in spite of hundreds of thousands on the streets saying No! No! No! on an island of only a few million, what did that signify? There was no *other* voice, nothing beyond the decided and the agreed-upon, there was nothing but the slap on the face. There *was* no country, just a handful of grey men in suits in a small tidy room with big windows and good coffee; there was nothing to which he owed a single moment of his life, a single drop of his blood, and yet drops of his blood slapped with small pat-pats on the roadway and dogs barked, a helicopter high in the air *butta-butta-ed*, women screamed and a big red-faced policeman was shouting *Don't arrest anyone local!* the country run by this order of rural wink-and-nod, farmers to each other over a hedge, God Bless America, the soldiers in battle fatigues crawling across the windows of the Departures Lounge like figures in a carnival, or about to walk on stage and perform some tarted-up modernised version of a Classical Greek play, *Antigone, Oedipus,* how would we live *without the beneficence of America?* and the beaten and the dead could fuck themselves; even as he fell under the first truncheon and there were marchers on a roof shouting through megaphones and playing, surreally, Bob Marley from a cheap cassette-recorder, he was thinking how absurd and rehearsed all of this was, and the newspaper's perky photographer had put his face in the pantheon of street-heroes of that useless, futile summer, a fine of three-hundred euros and don't let's mention what the police did, they were keeping public order and preventing criminal damage; – *even as he heard a women being judicially barred from ever entering that county again, prevented by a judge from walking on the earth of her own country, in the name of not embarrassing the Americans* – he was thanking God that he had not been sent to jail, the wound on his head was almost healed anyway, he dutifully paid the clerk and got out of the courtroom and the court buildings as quickly as he could, the doctor months later saying his depression might have been the result of a blow to the head but impossible to prove, but if he started to have those dark thoughts again even with the medication to come and see him sooner rather than later, whatever *later* meant. The doctor had no cure for what ailed him, he knew that, but he went to him because she was yelling at him, kicking his feet, groping in the nervous dark for his limp cock night after night, he'd nothing to give her. She'd left him because he couldn't fuck her and he spent all of his time watching TV like something killed, stuffed and propped against the side of the couch, something Norman Bates might hang on his wall; he was a hero in small rooms, snugs in some pubs, at least one girl had wanted to have him just because he'd been batoned; but it was over, dead, whatever it had been – you could talk about the soul, but why bother? – and he no longer cared who bombed who it was all the same in the end, you could waste your entire life saying No! to something or other, the weight of that was enormous, a fat slug in the chest moving about, slithering into the heart, you hated – as he did – every living thing in the end because everything was hopeless and the pills, at least, allowed him sporadic sleep, and he made his way to Dublin and they had one great celebratory or funerary piss-up, it might have been interpreted easily as one or the other, a girl cried in his lap and the following morning, rising from the still-drunkenly asleep girl whose name he could not remember or, more possibly, had never known, he was in a taxi in penitential rain making for the airport for no reason he could explain or motives he might fallibly dissect, it was a little like wondering at how a priest in a confessional had the power to forgive sins, trying to make out why he was in a taxi to a 'plane for the city of Paris where he'd never set foot before in his life.

All of this, of course, having happened to someone else at the dawn of all known time.

When he got back to his cell, a comfort in some ways, the square familiarity, his face was slapped again, this time by a used condom someone had hung above the door ingeniously so that when it opened there you were, the ammoniac seaweed stink and *Jesus Christ!* he could get AIDS; and he was on his knees tearing at his face when a guard, who was no stranger to jailed men cracking, found him on his knees making the sort of sounds the heartbroken or the dying make.

The *avocat* was not pleased that he had been unable to read his novel at lunchtime. This made him irritable.

The building in which he and others like him had their desks and duties dreamed of past glories, of a new Napoleonic plan for the world; and like a tired and defeated old man, peeled and creaked now in every pore. The wrought-iron balconies wore elegant garlands of rust and the exact and formidable blocks in the walls accrued dainty dandyish *boulevardier* scarves of damp. Below the window behind him, so close that on winter evenings it crackled and flashed like distant lightning, was a neon sign for a *brasserie*. Out of the horizon, over a skirt of green, strode the great prick of the *Tour Eiffel* and, if he turned his head, the cyclopean face of Notre-Dame de Paris shoved its awkward horns up over a cropped skyline of sloping windowed roofs. For months the great fanciful façade had dozed behind a veil of yellowish industrial netting and webbing and on the old lady's wrecked grey of the cathedral's face a new bright skin had emerged. There was, however, music.

The *avocat* launched his old-young body at an angle over the rusting balcony, aware, as always, of its fragility. He could smell the river, or imagined he could. The sounds of the street were mostly conversation; over it, like a layer of delicate and expensive cream, oozed this balm of music. In a waste basket near his right leg, someone had deposited a news-sheet; he glanced down and read *Spécialiste en Rénovation de l'Habitat – Traitement charp.....*

On an open space below him, four musicians played, a violin, a viola, another violin, and a young man squatting on a foldable chair nursed a cello between his knees. The cello-case lay open and invited donations. But the young men, slim and dressed in formal black, were intent on their music; something the *avocat* recognised but could not name. Of course: Pachelbel's *Canon*. Rightly, the young men, who seemed to the *avocat's* ears both technically proficient and fond of their music, had judged that something popular, at least well known, was what the street required. As each instrument slid into place atop the next and the graceful repeating and overlaying began, the *avocat* – and, perhaps, the very building he leaned from – began to hum the melody, that delicious and predictable descent and rise, that sense of order which existed in very few things these days. A scrum of bicycles gleamed unattended in the sunlight just outside the *brasserie;* he had a fleeting but nonetheless quite real desire to run down, mount one of them, and peddle away into as much distance as his strength would allow. With that sublime music in his ears. Some tourists passed, came back, took photographs of the musicians and donated nothing. He retreated, closed the big windows together, a little ashamed of himself.

Faidherbe was standing in front of his desk, working his white appearing-in-court V-shaped collar in his fingers like a nervous child with a piece of string. Faidherbe – distantly related, it was said, but how distantly no one knew, certainly *ancien régime* in his head anyway, to soldier, anthropologist, engineer, dreamer of French Empire, scourge of the Algerine, cutlass cartographer of black Africa, Louis Léon César Faidherbe, big country town boy made good – was older than the *avocat* by a dozen years, a completely bald and very tall man whom, it was said, had a sluttish wife who played around. His face was parched and bony, this was mistaken by some for proof of legendary military forebears, men who'd *lived for France* – sprinkling of Royalists, Catholics to a man, not that fond of the Revolution anyway – and he always looked undernourished and nervous. He constantly wanted something; whatever it was, he seemed always to ask you for something else. His thin bird-like fingers fussed on the collar.

"Hervé, how is our Irish friend? Treating him well, are we?"

"Due process of the law. What can I do for you?"

"Now, there's really no need....."

Faidherbe stopped himself. The *avocat* looked down at his desk, so strewn and untidy it resembled aeriel photos of a bomb site. The whole room, for that matter, was cluttered. Faidherbe continued:

"It's hardly surprising that the case is the talk of the town, Hervé. One Frenchman murdering another wouldn't matter a damn."

"I don't share your cynicism."

"A true *crime passionel* of the old school," prompted Faidherbe. "I understand he has no criminal record here."

A mobile phone went off somewhere, the ring-tone playing something hysterically happy. Faidherbe drew himself up to his full height. At this point, he put the collar into his

41

pocket like a priest putting away the Host. The *avocat*, who had pretended to bend over his desk, discovered for the very first time that someone, many, many years ago, had etched the initials 'G.C.' into the brown wood; tiny letters, almost too small to see. Polished into eternity, there they were. Fascinating!

"Well, I've just come to offer my assistance, as it were, anything at all, however small. Colleagues should, well, *colleague*, so to speak."

Faidherbe, in his tall thinness, looking as if he might tip over, a piece of precious sculpture by Lladro.

"I appreciate it. I must apologise for my snappiness, *Maître* Faidherbe."

Stung by the sudden formality, Faidherbe — and this is the point for which he was recognised by all — hesitated, opened his mouth as if to say something else, and scuttled away. That eternal request, that perpetual unasked question, hung again in the air. The tall man's thin back cased in its respectful but inexpensive black suit, pitched and rolled across the room, reflected in a few rotting, pocked mirrors, until it disappeared into them. The *avocat* tried to recall whether he'd seen notes or a file or anything marked formidably, 'Casier Judiciare Chargé.' No, his client had no criminal record in France, and he resented Faidherbe for having panicked him for a moment. He *had* checked all that sort of thing. He longed for a cigarette. Some of the long windows in the room were open but it was cloyingly hot.

"He's annoyed that he wasn't given a bit of the case, that's all."

With her cropped hair and dark eyes she resembled that actress in that film about Paris but older, the one Marcel *ooh-ed* and *aah-ed* over for weeks, a famous film, but now he couldn't recall its title. Marie nursed a bundle of brown files to her breast. She wore a shiny black top today and tight black trousers which revealed, though demurely, the lines of her womanly underwear. Her designer spectacles were thin strips of glass held in invisible frames. An attractive woman who now and then enjoyed pretending to be a teenager, the *avocat* thought; and again, was ashamed of himself.

"There will be others, Marie. I don't know why I was selected or why anyone should be jealous or want a piece of the action, so to speak. There *is* no action. I am defending him, that's all."

Marie leaned over and said what she always said:

"Why don't you let me make you dinner some evening? A glass of wine, no shop-talk, just friends for an evening. You can bring that beautiful boy, if you'd feel safer. You are so *intense*, Hervé. "

He looked up at her, his features consciously blank. Her eyes behind the little slips of glass were deep and her gaze direct and open, like the gaze of a child.

"Go away. I'm an old married man."

Not for the first time, he wondered why he had so few women friends. He didn't mind Marie's flirtations. He didn't really *like* women. He'd been told that was odd; Marcel said women and gay men always got on well together because one was not a sexual threat to the other, it was a game of safety, with unspoken rules...... Well, not so with Marie.

She would be back tomorrow, going through this ritual again. It would never stop, it was a relationship. Perhaps there were other desks at which she paused to have similar parry-and-thrust conversations and maybe this helped her with her loneliness – he had judged that she was lonely, and that's why all this sort of talk, even with a gay man – but he didn't notice. Her sensuousness, its obviousness, was not unappealing and it gave off the impression of being curiously genderless. Not for the first time, the *avocat* wondered fleetingly whether Marie had had affairs with women. She tapped the desk with a manicured nail on the end of a nicotined finger and the wrinkles in the skin of her hand were almost unnoticeable. Then she was gone. An attractive women, surely there was someone in her life? But how could one tell? And did it matter?The *avocat* was seized by a curious and dark premonition. Beyond the closed windows now, the music had stopped and there was a spatter of applause. He looked at his watch. He stood up abruptly and his chair made a sharp, ratty sound on the old polished planks of the floor. He 'phoned for a taxi. Marie moved across his line of sight and smiled at him, the files gone now, her hands free to balance a pert and openly suggestive office-walk. Men's heads turned from more than one desk. Why did she play with him? It was truly intolerable. He gathered a few things together and packed them into his briefcase. He knew he was watched as he made his way to the door. He was late, *Jesus Christ*, by almost half an hour. It would take at least that again to get over the city to the prison.

He was angry to be told that his client was unable to see him; much as a doctor might feel on being told a patient was feeling too well to be examined. He felt rebuffed and was surprised at himself, the unprofessionalism of such feelings. He asked questions and eventually, in a small room which stank of old cigarettes and which had no window the *avocat*, feeling a prisoner himself, received official medical word on the condition of the Irishman.

"*Sedated?*"

It was a ridiculously young medical orderly who stood in front of him. Again, those irrational feelings of being slighted; the emotions of a true *flaubertois*.

"It is absolutely nothing serious, I assure you. He was upset."

"Upset by what?"

With unconcealed impatience, the orderly told him.

"This is disgraceful. I'll have to make a note."

A shrug.

"This is a prison."

The *avocat* rose to his feet; how simple it was and how easy to lose one's dignity just by sitting down. The wooden

44

chair creaked as he rose into the cigarette smells. There were things he should say, of course, complaints, perhaps, to make, tables to be metaphorically thumped; but he was not up to the challenge. The orderly, without being asked, going through the motions of an enormous and endless dance, took him to see his client. He viewed the sleeping figure through the Judas. The whole business − of being a prisoner, of being sedated on a prison cot, of being slapped in the face with a used condom, of spying on a prisoner − well, it was just insufferable beyond words, nothing to do with being a human being at all, a functioning *person*. He was aware that the ancient jail housed − *why?* − the last guillotine in France. He had never asked to view it, though other braver young men of the law had, and they remarked that it was curious how there seemed not to be any bloodstains anywhere on the machine. He turned quickly to the orderly and, wordlessly, allowed himself to be led out of the cells.

Doors groaned open and locks clicked and clacked and he was out in the hot street, not in the least inclined to return to the office; there should have been a vague luxury, a schoolboy naughtiness, about taking time off for oneself. But as he walked away from the prison, he felt only a weighty fatigue, as if he were coming down with the 'flu. And his throat had constricted, as if he were very sad or very tense. He did not know what was happening to him.

A day's heat rose up out of the streets, turned the spoked iron guards at the base of trees into griddles upon which saints might be roasted alive, animated the gargoyles of shy, insignificant churches; taxi drivers shouted at one another, pretty girls sat on café chairs with their legs open under very short skirts and the crotches of their panties showing brazenly; blue here, white there, a deep black. Young men lounged back in designer jeans and slacks, busy or expectant, on display; executives skipped through traffic with the agility of champion soccer-players and patent leather wallets dangled from their wrists; cobbled streets with their drains like spines running down the middle, ancient and humming with heat, bristled under the gossipy stonework of venerable houses and Sun King apartments, now boutiques and jewellery stores.

He found himself at a small round table outside a café in God only knew where, fiddling uselessly with his novel. He ordered a Turkish, and when it came its black thick mix of pure sugar and coffee rattled his nerves. A delivery van drew up in front of him; the sign-work depicted a row of naked men, their backs and arses to him, in loud black-and-white. Then it was gone, as if some bizarre strip show had appeared and disappeared before his eyes and just for him, or perhaps he'd imagined it.

Feeling his eyelids droop, the *avocat* found comfort in a sweet child's daydream of a true Lyon *bouchon* where he could eat at all hours of the day, food cooked on the spot, *cochonaille* with everything, sausages fat and filling wrapped in pig's intestines, potato-herring in a slavering oil, black pudding, *rognons;* a friendly crowd in, no one knowing anyone else but a banter going on, a homeliness, the city of Saint-Exupéry and The Little Prince, not the butcher's shop of Klaus Barbie; in this *bouchon-*of-the-imagination, a fat friendly proprietress would ask him how he was getting on, how were his law studies going, was his father proud? His mother – had the tests come back? He will not know himself in Paris if he moves there, not like here. Saint-Éxupery made a very close swing over the angled rooftops and the Lumière brothers filmed it all.....

"M'sieu'."

"What?"

"Pardon me, M'sieu', but you were falling asleep. We thought you were drunk."

He opened his eyes and in the sky saw the crop-bearded face of an elegant waiter whose large brown eyes stared into his. He quickly straightened himself up, looked at his watch; a respectable man who'd done something embarrassing in public. Already a mysterious and bitter coolth had crept into the air; as if winter had come, and he'd missed the rest of the

46

year. An empty plate of something or other sat before him; clearly he had eaten, but he couldn't remember it. The world was playing silly tricks on him.

"Bill, please. And, by the way, I'm tired, not drunk."

The waiter went away without any comment. When he looked around him, the *avocat* saw that there were no other customers at any of the tables, that he was quite alone – how they must have laughed at him through the windows of the sinister little café on the rue-Who-Gives-a-Fuck! Then he discovered that his throat was sore. He stood up. The waiter came out with rehearsed dignity and handed him his bill. He paid, took up his briefcase, walked off, leaving the change.

Now and then the peephole vision of the Irishman lying on his cot came back to him, but it was like a car with its headlights off ploughing at him through a thick fog, and he was very glad indeed when he hailed down a taxi.

He had slept well. He did not want to ascend from the warm drugged pool into which they'd thrown him; their arms upon him, restraining him, he remembered that first of all, there might be a bruise or two, the mark of a strong finger. He lay on his back, chemically content, and Arab music floated over the acid air of his cell, distant, haunting, high-pitched and fast; then it stopped and he heard, mutedly, a voice speaking rapidly; a radio, someone had a radio in his cell, someone heard the outside world. But it was no different, really, from hearing sounds drifting over the prison walls from a world which, with every passing minute, was ceasing to exist; a spurt of nerves, then a slowing-down of the heart, whatever they'd given him worked well.

He pissed yet again but awkwardly on the squat, the smell stung his nostrils; sound outside and the smell, an acrid sense of interference, upsetting, but nothing to be done about it; he sat back on his cot, ignored a small table opposite, a plain chair. But they'd taken pity on him, and someone had left him two unopened packs of Silk Cut and a lighter, which must be against the regulations, the possibility that he might set fire to the cot, himself; but someone had taken the chance, and he snatched up a packet, ripped open the cellophane and got a cigarette into his mouth – his mouth tasted stale, sticky and hot – and lighted it as if they were about to snatch everything away from him; but the Judas slid open and shut several times in what he took to be a very few minutes, and no one came in, no one did anything, he was left alone. It occurred to him that someone sat outside, reading or thinking or staring at a wall, vaguely protecting himself from himself. He tried to imagine this person, fat or thin, young or middle-aged, nearing pensioned retirement perhaps, tired of his work: listening for telltale sounds, listening and not listening at the same time, absorbed in his own private world yet responsible for the safe continuation of his. This sense of being reluctantly protected, if indeed it was based in any truth, comforted him. He sat back with his head against the wall, remembered the hanging condom, but it was not there now. No one would threaten him now, his invisible guardian outside – he was so sure of him now, was that the sound of someone breathing? Or some hiss, merely, from a radio at the end of the universe?

Oh, he knew how it worked! Orders would have come down – always *down?* why not *up?* – that there were to be no more incidents, nothing likely to cause protests between legal men in suits, embassies, consulates, ambassadors, countries. Nothing that might cause a journalist to come around, rat-nose sniffing; that's how it was done, the threat of names in newspapers, read out on the radio – perhaps it was happening right now, on that radio whose garble and warble he could hear, in a language he could not adequately understand – faces on TV. Odd and ironic how one nameless – but he *had* a name – Irishman could cause an entire apparatus to sit up and take note; make changes, alter its behaviour. It was what they'd always said was possible, though, perhaps to be truthful, he'd believed very little of it. In the squalid brown-smoked pubs, the backrooms of pubs, that one person was all it took to change a world, any world, one voice could shout louder than a hundred cannon, look at Tiananmen Square, one man, jacket trailing the ground, and that ugly, stopped tank; sophistry, drinks slopping on the fag-end floor, wanting only to fuck the nearest girl at the table, politics a sideshow to the real game of getting laid. Or so she had accused him, even before she could not live with him any longer; she seeing the game within the game, the hubris of ever thinking a group such as theirs could change *any*thing, that sort of uninformed pride belonged to adolescents and they were not that, some of them distinctly, even he could see it, past some sort of biological or mental Sell By date, childless women driven to mothering a Cause, men who drank too much and were violent anyway given a Cause in which they could hate safely; but it was unfair to say they were all like that because he wasn't, they weren't. But where were all the really pretty girls? Why did they stay away?

The Arab music came on again, he tapped his ash on the floor of the cell and closed his eyes and he was running, the painter standing in the doorway, light behind him, a sort of ikon, he'd been with the girl and the girl had him by the hand: the painter, dyed hair back-lit, a flame, it was all a movie now, was shouting at them, he'd been drinking wine all evening, *Try not to screw her! Don't bring her back too stoned!* Most pathetic of gestures: the painter had grabbed weakly at his sleeve – what would a punch from those ringed hands achieve? - and pointed to a rough newspaper portrait of a squat, bald little man high on the far wall, among the thousand torn-out reproductions, the pinned-up articles, a forest of visual and literary information, most of it useless – *There! Max Jacob! He's my hero.* The painter just had to look at him with those sad Semite's eyes to know he had never heard of him, didn't understand. Then looking quickly at the girl, shrugged him free: *Saw a vision of Christ and became converted. He was bent as a three-pound, but never mind. We all flirt with angels once in a while.* Was he about to start weeping? There was a fragile gaiety in his voice, as if he were sending them off to their deaths and didn't wish to think about it too much, that voice that contained too many accents and none, a joke made into the air at the edge of a pit, this Jew who said he'd been un-Jewed but then what defined it? *Go,* said the painter: *Fuck off! With my blessing!* He turned his back on them.

He and the girl out in the night, both steadying in its chill, she stands in the middle of the street, a slim butt of a thing, like a bone wrapped in gauze, flagging down a taxi, he not knowing quite what he's doing there, amazed at himself to be doing such an ordinary thing in Paris, as if he'd suddenly awakened in a strange but not unfriendly room, this street, turn, this, a run, then the taxi – you sit only in the back seats – rushing through what appeared through the windows to be a gaudily lit village of old buildings, inelegant, due for resculpting, a sign, an indicator: Butte aux Cailles. The wheels of the taxi rumbling on cobblestones, everything on a slight descent, a 'plane making a final approach, Paris with wings, towards the river, the sound of *rai* coming from somewhere and a lot of people about, everything fleeting and fast and exciting in an indescribable way, not knowing where you were being taken in such a James Bond city being part of what life's all about, after all, a beautiful mysterious woman by your side; suddenly swooping like a bird with eyes all round its square head down on the silvery black mirror surface of the river, such traffic and such speed, such unhesitancy, past shuttered shops, doors, windows, then lights of many hues, a dream happening within a dream within the taxi itself, was her hand still resting upon his?

The four proud towers of the Bibliothèque Nationale reflected speedily the sparkling air, this Ariel aspect, his own Caliban staring through the reflection of himself on the window glass, hovering high up and over the rooftops like a warning; so far up in the air you can go, like a Tower of Babel, he thought to himself, but the taxi was somewhere else now, and the river was beneath them, or they were flying above the river and the taxi's radio was on, Arab lutes and electric guitars. A dizzy feeling, nothing like it since he'd been a pimple-poxed adolescent, of stumbling upon accidental adventures, simple things in themselves but loaded with significance, symbols of worlds behind worlds, you unbalanced yourself for a moment and there, behind the curtain, a new landscape lay and glistering galleons from Carthage swooned moored in the crescent moon-shaped harbours of your cascading imagination. Better than good dope, such innocence, such flung-wide openness.

She grasped his hand, a warm, damp, child's grip; he opened his eyes, the cigarette had burned down to his fingertips, the cell door was open, that yellow hallway light like spilt ice-cream on concrete.

A not unfriendly voice told him his lawyer had called to see him earlier, but he had been asleep. It would not have been appropriate to waken him.

A sign above the carriage door said: ***10 ans de poésie,*** and underneath it, three lines by someone whose name she could not make out. The carriages rocked and the brakes and wheels flinted around the curves and canters of the world beneath the city. Here the Nijinski-nimble pickpockets danced, two to a team, each with his territory and duty; one man to pretend to board the train, who'd then snatch a wallet, back-step as the doors closed, walk slowly up the platform, hand the find to an accomplice, who'd walk in the opposite direction, the first man then exiting the stage up the steps into the open air. Almost beauty.

Here people lived, slept, ate and robbed unseen by those who came down merely to catch a train. Beyond the electronic stile, opened by the grabbing insertion of a ticket – but the young African men could leap the stiles ticketless – under the

51

great arcing advertisements, the grinning models, the holidays in exotic locations, the brilliant comedy shows – what did laughter sound like? – photo exhibitions of Paris before George Eugène Haussmann, Prefect of the Seine, false Baron, pulled down the house he'd been born in to remake Paris, a symbol if ever there was one; the idiotically beaming children slurping variflavoured drinkable yoghurt, a universe of events, full of flesh and imagination and feelings, moved about oblivious to the jerking trains.

She knew this world and the hardness of the plastic chairs to sleep on, the interruptions – the contempt on the faces that leered down, uniformed and smug – and the fear as the rats populated the sinewy caverns in the black stinking hours of the morning; or how flesh began to smell as it roasted on spits of electric currents. How one world, several worlds, played tick-tack with the world of ordinary things, unnoticed, the taps on the shoulder unfelt as things invisible giggled by. How each minute above ground was a miracle.

She sat on a treacherous little orange seat that she'd had to pull down, against its own resisting strength, and sit on before it flapped up again; in front of her sat a very fat Arab woman, bags about her feet and a fading blue tattoo on that part of the bridge of her nose which blended into her forehead, that mixture of disdain and aloofness; against the door rested an elegant Japanese man in a dark suit carrying a briefcase, swaying gently like a fake flower driven by a tiny clockwork mechanism. The carriage began to fill up; station to station, more people got on than got off, and she felt her chest tighten. Now and then, as if to reassure herself that all journeys have an end – even though propped up on a cushion of fluffy comfort by the few commonplace downers she'd managed to score – she'd glance at the Métro map on the curve of the wall, a thing curiously resembling a diagram she'd once seen in one of the painter's books of the arteries and veins of the human arm. It was while staring at the map, her eyes stiffening there in the drugged intensity of her gaze, that a monstrous face loomed over her out of the very bowels of the carriage.

Startled, she gave a tiny involuntary jerk back in her seat. She put both hands lightly across her bag. The Arab woman smiled. Above what had become a small hedge of twitching legs and bodies a wide red mouth begged something of the world; then a rabbit with thin, frayed ears, joined in. Where had her mind wandered? A carriage-performer had drawn a black sheet across the end of the carriage – gone, now, those ten years of poetry – and from behind the sheet was working grotesque hand-puppets. Their lips were made of wood and did not move, so whatever was uttered meant nothing to her. The red mouth was chopped into a yellow head and topped off with a stark upright brush of black hair. The head snapped right, left, there was some bulging of the black sheet. She saw that not one face in the portion of the carriage she could see turned to acknowledge in any way the existence of the puppets. Perhaps she was the only one who could see them? Her nerves jangled a little and she felt in her pocket for the comfort of the scrap of tissue paper in which her last few pills were wrapped. Something to let her sleep, that was all. She had no plans, no method. The future extended no farther than the black sheet on top of which the puppets, like infantile gods, made their epileptic girations. Soon enough the gods were gone, and the puppet-master was pushing his way about, his mouth moving, beseeching, red like the mouths of his dolls.

She felt a great weight of disappointment move, as pregnant girls said their babies moved, in her belly. The past was a picture-show, an illumination too vivid to behold for long; sleep, drowsiness, wrapped the pictures in a light but impenetrable gauze. She could smell herself, and knew she needed a good bath – the painter had bathed her, hadn't he? His fat stained fingers soaping her back, the water in that ancient cracked bath warm and thick and soapy and he'd gone out, sometimes, into the milling *puces* markets and brought back imitation scents in phials and sometimes he'd pour them over her back, run his fingers along the bumps of her spine, take particular care over the flowering bruise here, the redness there, his marks, his imprints, rubbing in the oils, the scents, the soap, as if that alone might remove them.

Such moments with him were luxurious, before the young man came, those days of delicious alteration between black and white, green and blue, holiness and happiness, the fierce passion of his beatings when his cock would not stay filled or when she'd do or not do something – what were, after all, the rules? – and the ugly grimace of him when she'd jiggle his timid little bird in its grey-and-black nest until it spat a few glutinous drops; had it been all she'd wanted in the world? The young man had appeared like a great fullstop to a rush of soundless words that had no beginning and no planned end.

She decided, haphazardly guessing where she was, to get off. She was pushed out onto the platform by the force of the Arab woman behind her and some others. It was good to feel the indifference of people, to know that she went unnoticed once again in the world.

For there was never any point consciously in hiding. The living, moving world could hide you well enough. A push, then, through the silvery swing-doors and up the steps into a flash of city traffic and the smell, always, of exhausts and cigarettes and the underground world. As if the city of Paris had let go of a silent fart, like a kid in church! She grinned, a small girl, thin, quite smartly if casually dressed, and pretty too, balanced for a couple of moments on the lip of a Métro station, framed in ornate green metal, crowned with the great green word, *Métropolitain*. On either side of her walked, with great pride, beautiful half-African, one-third-Asian, one-quarter-Arab people, men and women made beautiful by this subtle old blending, citizens of a world within a world within a world, the young and old inhabitants of the city where, tonight, unlike them, she had neither home nor name.

In the window of a shuttering café, as the waiters removed the tables and chairs from outside, one waiter arguing with a small, impeccably dressed man who appeared to have fallen asleep into his plate, a sad clown grinned at her, chin in hand, from a poster; on either side of him rested, work done, blackboards advertising salads and coffee and baguettes and finished lunches. She watched the small neat man stand up unsteadily, look around him like a child who had trespassed into a neighbour's garden. Under the peeling corruption of a high gable wall an ancient advertisement struggled through: a smiling man holding a fish, *Chez Emile BOUSSUGE Ain...* the rest of the announcement trailing into the years. Everything lived discreetly under everything else.

As she approached the train station, a great cathedral of a place out of which people dribbled forth as if reluctant to leave, taxis hobbling here and there, she saw already some dark shapes huddled in black coats and gaudy blankets, even bits of cardboard, on the steel grilles above the air vents of the Métro – all over the city, she knew, people were doing this, sucking up the sickly heat, fighting each other for a place early in the afternoon – and others hung around the reaching arms and legs of the train station, a heart among hearts whose arteries began and ended on the edge of the world for all she knew. In among the great pillars of a railway bridge figures moved clumsily and bantered, black figures, colour and race meaningless in the bleak democracy of these dark places. Past a group of such men scampered a lovely young girl, well dressed, carrying a baby in her arms, trotting along like a refugee from a bombardment. The men did not look up and the girl did not look back.

She decided against the pillars. She did not want to risk a drunken rape and besides, there was talk for some time about how you could be spirited off by men who had no morals, who traded in cheap white girls like herself. The younger the better, of course; but on lampposts and walls everywhere there remained the flapping ruins of posters with innocent girls' faces on them, the age of the girl, the name, though that was often false:

'Last seen at..... 'It was understood, without much comment, that the girls were already dead. 'Missing' only applied to people in the ordinary world. So she decided against the pillars.

Not having any covering worth the name, she made her way into the station, a place suddenly so open and so vast and, even at this hour, so apparently crowded that nothing could ever hide in it. Several tracks were empty of trains. Departure-Arrivals boards flicked over like eyelids. The café was closing, but it was a possibility. A final coffee. She walked quickly, past the shuttered shops and the One-Minute photo-booths and felt around her feet the blown rags of newspapers whose news was very, very old.

She sat the bar of the café, alone. The mirror of the bar reflected her face between the bottles and glasses and stick-on adverts: on some of these, smiling girls' faces, brightly enhanced, had, she thought, the flat skin texture of patients heavily doped.

"We're closed, M'zell'."

His lips barely moved, so that what she read came to her as:

"....zed, 'Zell."

She looked at him, a neatly turned out young black man with his hair impeccably done up and dyed like wheat-stalks in rows. He was handsome, his eyes were black rather than brown, his skin shone in the neon glare; in one corner of the mirror, just above his head, a plastic red rose flashed on and off brilliantly, like a signal, from a tiny bulb in its heart; but he hadn't the least interest in her. He washed and stacked glasses, sorted bright white coffee cups, he turned his back upon her. He was done with her, but she knew he watched her in the mirror; at night, one could never be sure, she might have a knife.

She slipped down off the stool. Behind her the empty vastness of the station was pocked with the figures of men knocking off work, black men in a hurry here and there, the occasional pale face appearing like an absence, Arab women in blue smocks moving slowly along behind trolleys. Even if one came close and she caught the movement of her lips, the words meant nothing to her. She felt the coldness lick her heart, but it was a familiar feeling and she was prepared for it.

She made her way along a platform, the stink of the empty tracks comforting. For no reason at all she turned abruptly and left the station; in a doorway blazing with posters advertising rock-concerts and gay clubs and Roumanian girls offering massages, *Nis good end claen,* she swallowed down a dry throat a couple of her pills. She walked away slowly, knowing precisely how long it took for the pills to kick in and calculating also that they would go down on a cushion of pills taken earlier; such were the kinds of mathematics in which she had become expert. Now when she reached the pillars again she had no fear, and the figures moving around her made her feel nothing at all; neither did any speculations of violation or sudden death or the acquisition of disease. Leaning against the grey-painted hard foot of an enormous pillar in a temple of pillars she felt the distances, the gaps between each one harden and become as impenetrable as a wall of iron. Now she was herself, in her own place. When she thought of the painter there was no image beyond his face. She giggled lightly, looking around her like an impish schoolgirl. The streetlights were like oranges hanging on invisible threads from an invisible ceiling; taxis fled past as if leaving a burning city. At midnight the bells of the church of St-Vincent de Paul sounded out quickly, but she didn't hear them.

The flashy but depressing shops on the Goutte d'Or had closed their steel eyelids, and on the hill where the city's first bishop, Saint Denis, was beheaded, picking up his head, walking off with it under his arm, the turn into a new day came as a warm breeze pushing upwards through the trees around the Square and overweight American women sweated in pullovers with *Moulin Rouge* and a transfer of a windmill spread across mountainous chests as they struggled up out of café chairs. The portrait merchants and artists who could cut your profile out of paper as you stood in front of them were packed away and gone.

She pulled her knees to her chest, a child not yet born; and uncovered, she curled like a myth among those enormous reeds of steel.

A soft hot rain had begun to hiss along the sloping street; the taxi's wipers were on, *shoo-ish, shoo-ish, shoo-ish,* the street began to look as if it were made of glass.

They took it in turns, some nights Marcel's place, some nights his, and tonight he was glad of the comfort of the approach of his big cracking wooden front doors, their appalling unnecessary majesty. Not with a key, with its memories of a larger age, but with a feeble electronic button, he opened them.

The hallway had its usual chill, and that too in a way was comforting; the high ceiling, the crawling wrought-iron banisters ascending like Jacob's Ladder into some sort of heaven, the squat grey block of postboxes with their intimate little name-tags: he opened his box, nothing in it but circulars. Disappointed – why did he always expect, with a child's rush of excitement, that the postbox would one day hold the secret to redemption and happiness? – he looked briefly at the stairs. One always lived in fear of attack, it was the times. Perhaps it had always been *the times.* He turned right past what once had been the concierge's vigilant roost, and opened the front door, with much meddling of keys and three turns here and one there, to his ground-floor apartment. For this he paid through the nose. A modest but adequate kitchen space was set off to the left of the hall and beside it the bathroom and toilet, spacious at the expense of a decent-sized kitchen. In the kitchen itself, Marcel had arranged all the cutlery – the knives were Avabard, the very best, they didn't stretch to that in the restaurant where he worked! – in tidy racks, his National Service time doing him some good, as he put it: his had been intolerably miserable, a time of exquisite loneliness and forbidden urges in a barracks crammed with angry homophobic men.

The place was impeccably ordered. There was a general purposes closet, full of brooms, cleaning liquids and that sort of thing, set in flush to the right, then the big, airy bedroom, with a window that nudged wickedly on to the street; on hot lazy Sundays he and Marcel lay there with one side of the window open, the street sounds swallowing them up, the room smelling of sex and the white flimsy curtains billowing in the hot breeze, hoping someone would peek in and be outraged; Marcel would put on some loud music, too. But nothing ever happened. The bed was large and covered in a blue fluffy throw, and the pillows had small *khamsa* designs – like the hands of children – at their edges, a birthday present from Marcel.

A large bamboo groped sloppily upwards in the corner, the walls were a blinding white, not easy to keep clean, you only had to rub against them, and there were mirrors, sensible and horizontal, set where they could watch each other in bed. Books and magazines lay on the floor, careless and elegant, and the ceiling was very high.

The *avocat* possessed one big living room, the ceiling high and white, the walls decorated in African masks and expensively framed posters advertising long-dead Art exhibitions: Signac, Kupka, and one by Gilgogué, designated in bold black letters, *en permanence*. He flicked the wall switches and the room was warmed by hesitant, pale light. He turned on quickly his expensive, compact sound-system, he detested silence in empty rooms, and immediately, in gentle but resonating currents of music, the first notes of Bach's *Allemande*, Suite No. 1 in D Minor, fluttered out from beneath the dead fingers of Glenn Gould. This *flaubertois* had worked hard to sophisticate himself; he chuckled, the sound mocking and slightly scary in the room. He put down his briefcase on the deep, cream leather sofa, it could double as a bed for visitors, and noticed the flicking green eye of the answering machine beside the silver slimline telephone on a steel-legged table upon which also resided a small flatscreen TV. *You asked to be kept informed. She has slipped in to a coma. If you would like to come over?*

From the first day she'd complained, till now, seemed like his whole life. His father had *gone before her,* as she quaintly, and unsatisfactorily, explained it to him, and to herself. Operation had piled upon operation like so many assaults at Verdun. So many futile recuperations after that – the generals too far back from the Front Line to be as knowledgeable as they might have been. Years passed, the woman refused to follow her husband, his father, and he had come to resent her for still being alive. This, in turn, gave him the guilt he needed to endure her. Every now and then, one of these calls, the aftershock hanging in the air like a deadly gas, affecting his nerves; the last decade had not been kind, they had not been kind to each other. His mother was a demanding woman, sad to have only one child, her womb ripe and full, too eager for the countrywoman's large family her sisters – his jolly, healthy aunts – had jettisoned into the world. From her silent, withering couch in an expensive tree-muffled hospice – yes, he resented that, the loose flow of money, the things he couldn't do because of it, and Marcel resented it too and said so, which sounded more cruel than it actually was – she ruled him still, refusing, when she had still been conscious, ever to see Marcel, whom she did not consider a man: and, by implication, she didn't consider her son Hervé a man either. For spite, now and then she'd slip into a coma, demanding from that blackness that he attend upon her. On good days she remembered her own father – thinking her son was her father – jumping on the back of a two-wheeled hay-cart in full uniform to go off to have his face blown away; he'd slit his wrists in the Red Cross field tent. How old *was* his mother, anyway? *Papa! Your little Lulu, Papa!*

He poured himself a glass and considered the drive. The car could do with exercise, give it a run in the country.

He'd go into the private garage – it belonged to residents of the building – and turn the engine over. He wouldn't bring Marcel.

The Irishman intrigued him. His insistence that he didn't kill the older man had brought the case to a head, like squeezing on a pimple. It appeared clear enough, by the evidence at least. Well, that is to say, it looked virtually impossible *that he was not culpable.* Mitigation, of some sort; there was possibly something to be had there. All the work. Crime of passion. The girl. Rage. Jealousy.

On an impulse, he took his cassette-recorder from his briefcase and switched it on. His client's voice echoed around the room like the voice of a ghost: *At first I didn't know who it was. I leaned over him......*

The *avocat* dropped himself into the comfort of the expensive leather couch, glass in hand. Red wine from a bottle already opened and vacuum-recorked – by Marcel? Bach fluttered on, hysterical notes, and the lovable irritation of Gould humming, another ghost. Like his mother. A ghost-in-flesh. So who did you *think* it was, if at first you didn't think it was *him*, that huddle at the bottom of the stairs to his bedroom, his secret place?

The *avocat's* ruminations slid away on a wetness round his fingers; he had allowed his glass of red wine to tip, bloody blotches flecked through the hairy cream pile of a small carpet which ran along the front of the couch. Cursing, he placed his glass on a side table made of an elegant turning and varnishing of a slab of Irish bog-oak; standing up, he allowed the cassette to run on as he floundered out to the kitchen for a towel, a damp cloth, anything; he knew the stain was there until something more chemical and professional might be done about it.

In the kitchen, beside the sink, he found a novel by Fawzi Mellah. No, not his. Marcel's, then. He flung himself back into the living room; Gould above the softer plaints of his own bad English and the voice of the young Irishman: *Then there was the wine bottle on the ground. In pieces.* His own voice then: *Blood and wine.* Why had he said that? Because in the dark light of the painter's courtyard, and from a short distance, he'd been over it several times, blood and wine would look the same? *Like a dark red shining halo.*

You see all that blood, the *avocat* thought, padding fruitlessly at the carpet with a damp cloth; you see all the blood, a dark shining, the blood and wine, a murderous transubstantiation: yet it's late and you are standing – where? All you can decide is that he might be drunk? No attempt to help himself more thoroughly, to provide something more substantial. As if his innocence were incidental, or unnecessary. Curious. A fall *could*, of course, have occurred. Three of them, sharing that space, one offering himself up, one becoming invisible..... a place of magic, perhaps, a sacrifice had to be made......

His ineptitude with the glass had made him tetchy, the stains were not fading and he was making things worse. Pieces of piano-music, fragments of the young man's speech, shards of his own: he lay back on the couch, the tape ran out, Gould concluded his prodding of Bach and he was glad of the silence. The high ceiling gave him a sort of distance to look up towards. Perhaps he dozed. Marcel woke him up, flamboyant, showy, camp, dressed in a very loud shirt to the collar of which was pinned a large round badge with the face of Marilyn Monroe pouting from it. Marcel was humming now, moving from the kitchen to the living room, saying *tut-tut* things about the mess on the carpet, then, without breaking his rhythm, bending and rolling it up – a sharp nostrilling of something by Issey Miyake – *You just can't be left alone for two minutes, can you, my heart? Piddles on the carpet!* – all that sudden campness routine just a tad hard to handle this hour of the morning, what time was it?

For no reason he could think of, but perhaps the heart has its reasons and so forth, the *avocat* heard himself say, as if he were another man, in another room, or standing, perhaps, just over his own shoulder, *Since when have you taken to reading North African novels?*

The Second Day

She held his hand, the street lamps seemed to shine down from a very great height, a weak, watery shining. There was a wall made of corrugated iron, a dog barking in the distance, weeds growing up between the stones and broken pavement; blocks of flats, high, shaking now and then from a shout or a blow of loud music, and the impudent rattle of a train somewhere in the stale air. They walked among figures who were vaguely human, who became shadow, changed their shape, teased him with their sniggering at jokes he could not comprehend and in that incomprehensible coded slang. Here and there a baseball cap, peak turned backwards or sideways, eased itself forward; beneath it he could at first see nothing in the bubbling dark, then the forms of the face would gather, the black eyes, the thick lips, the uncannily white teeth. They moved about in a sort of graceless dance, trousers baggy, as if they'd shat themselves or been caught running out of a lavatory. Yet she was comfortable here and if they eyed him, her presence reassured them; she made quick signs with her fingers and they knew, they knew with an intelligence livelier than his what it was she desired, these shadow-players, dark-skinned and mysterious and dangerous, ageless in their youth.

With a jolt of panic he understood that she had brought him along to be her strong arm, her armour; what an absurd idea! He didn't even symbolise these identities, and as often as possible he strolled away from these wiry, fast-shifting youths in their mock-American ghetto dress, these unreal, made-up people, who were not themselves but someone else, who had

63

become what they envied, without a moment's introspection and no regret. Small things moved from hand to hand out of a street darkness so deep and thick it might have been made of oil. Satisfied, she hugged her seller, he shrugged and shoulder-danced back with the others, into a dark that swallowed up even the pale peak of his cap; someone turned on a radio and the music was a beat, a single rhythm, and a man's voice so angry it was, to his ears, tragic. He was glad to cross the suicide-bombed-looking street; he was glad to see newspapers blowing here and there and the sound of a steady rush of traffic not far away, and the headlines of some of the blown-apart newspapers containing one word, *Bush*, which he did not have to translate. Then she turned round and for no reason slapped him in the face so hard he woke up.

The doctor, he recognised him, was patting his cheek. Over the doctor's sports-jacket shoulder a yellow sword of light fell from the ceiling; the door of his cell was open. The doctor seemed happy enough, stood back a little, said something to the guard in the doorway. He had been in the street, in a city struck by bombs and ravaged by indefinable plague and now he was back here, on his cot, and the door was open – the guard's shadow could be seen, like a blanket rumpled up, blowing against the wall of the hallway – and the doctor, running his hand over the back of his head as if he was trying out a new haircut, said something to him in brusque French and went out. He tried for a moment or two to catch the last phrases of his dream, or recollection, whatever it was, but he could not.

He had gone out that evening with the girl, she had taken him along and made the painter jealous, of his youth, perhaps, he never felt youthful, and she had satisfied herself with some dope, taken out a small makeshift device, a bottle as tiny and elegant as an antique perfume glass, they'd been squatting down in a doorway that smelled of urine against a ravaged door once elegant, and taxis had passed by more slowly than he had ever seen them before and he took another – his first? – sip from the pipe and the back of his head tried to detach itself from

64

its duty to cover the brain and his stomach rolled and he threw up, the girl making some kind of noise for laughter, the bile in his stomach green and slimy, his eyes watering but already he couldn't feel any sensation in his feet.

Someone brought coffee, the coffee was sweet and heavily sugared. They wanted to bring him round, to flush out what the doctor had pumped into him, why was that? But he drank the coffee to the sugary dregs and then a hand appeared – out of the cell wall? – and gave him his cigarettes. He had been vomiting all over his shoes, somewhere in the unreal background, over the roofs, the skinny trees, the apartment blocks, a child's voice was shouting *Les Bleus! Les Bleus!* Maddeningly surreal, a colour shouted on the stinking night air, the doorway smelt like a graveyard, rot and growth, the girl slapping him on the back, tears rolling down her wonderful, powder-puff, lemon-meringue cheeks, he had run his hand along her thigh and dug his fingers deep into the seam of her trousers just where her crotch was and she had not resisted. She had leaned her head down, his hand now finding her back, and opened his trousers and sucked up his cock with her small mouth enlarging like the mouth of a devouring fish and her head had moved up and down lightly, lightly, her tongue running his cock-head round and round, cleaning him, her fingers finding his balls, he grabbed for the glass bottle, the pipe, sucked, felt his balls explode in her hands and a rush of such force that he had to yell, had to, out of the darkness as her head moved more quickly and her brow furrowed, the pumping going on forever, and when he woke up she'd done up his trousers and lay sleeping with her head on his shoulder in that hideous doorway and a light rain falling, rainbowed by the headlamps of taxis crawling by, no one looking at them, a whole city somewhere over their shoulders and no one knowing them, or caring.

A guard brought him, wordlessly, a newspaper. He would have liked to see some mention of his case, even with his bad French he couldn't find one, only a photo of a British soldier, you could tell by the flag on the side of the tank, leaning out to shake hands with a group of men who, arms reaching up to him as if one touch would cure them of something hitherto hopeless, formed a mediaeval picture of peasants craving bread from a lord on horseback. Basra: even the black-and-white photo showing how hot and hard the sun was there, how everything was black or white, the camera could not lie.

He lay the paper aside and fell into a deep dark dreamless slumber.

She thought for a moment – how long is a moment? – that it was him, his hand coming through the clouds, his face enormous, bigger than the sky, brighter than the sun, lifting her, *Talitha cumi!* from the dead, a phrase remembered and confused from the convent school, as when Peter raised the daughter of Dorcus he had said *Tabitha, cumi!* and *tabitha* was the girl's name, Aramaic for gazelle, fleetfoot, lithe, graceful, she was a gazelle, said the sweet-faced nun, putty-skinned, looking at her with watery eyes, staring as a man stares, she thought it was the painter coming back for her, himself raised from the dead, the stone rolled away.

It was a dream, of course, or it was where she had been before she had emerged into the iron-and-diesel clamour of the early morning, the figures stirring around her, the coughing, the groaning, the shivering under cardboard, and the stench of glaucous stools and the vomiting of the wine drunks: *Talitha cumi!* So that when once a man had approached her and asked her her name she'd said Tabitha, and he'd stood back and mouthed *You fucking Arab cunt!* And he'd slapped her and kicked her and walked away like a man going home for his lunch. She was not an Arab, but that was neither here nor there. Then again, she didn't know where she came from, so he might have been right, for all she knew. Her bag was still with her, a satchel of sorts. She'd slept with her head on it. She made her way into the train station, a city in itself already awake and moving quickly, no time to wait for anything or anyone, fast, pushy, a rash of trolleys and people with anxious faces; in the toilet she washed her face in evil-smelling green soap from a pushy dispenser until she smelled like a hospital ward, and dried her hair under the hot-air fan, stooping down at an awkward angle, ignoring the women who came in, vanished into closets and emerged to wash their hands or throw aside little crushed tissues. She too went into a closet, pissed, saw the first red paint-slash on the crotch of her knickers, went out again, put coins in a wall-dispenser, bent herself double in a cubicle again, inserted the tampon, wrestled a little with it, took off her knickers, stuffed them behind the toilet-bowl, produced a clean pair from her bag, slipped into them, wiped herself once more for luck, pulled up her jeans and went out and washed her hands again; a tousle-haired puck-faced doll ready for the day. She swallowed a small yellow pill and calmed down. Pictures were sliding into her head – a slide show she could neither prevent nor predict – which she could well do without and whose immensity could do her harm, rob her of vital energy, and the day had only begun. She went into the station again, up to the counter of the same café she'd been refused at the night before, this time a tall white boy watched over it, and he gave her, with a fetching smile, an espresso and a croissant and a packet of Silk Cut. She pointed at a row of Screwball Lotto cards. Already the stubs of dead cards lay at her feet; everyone tried his and her luck, the world was strange, you could arrive for coffee nearly black penniless at this counter and walk away a millionaire. Two smiling clown-faces, two dice, and the numbers 4 and 9. Nothing. But for a moment, for less than the blink of an eye, she had balanced on the edge of something delicious and threatening.

So no luck, p'teet?

Sitting alone, so he was trying her. Why not? The early morning, she smelt of lavatory soap, he was no fool, had seen them all in her, girls like her. She stirred three sugar cubes into her pitch-black coffee. She liked the way his lips moved, wet, like a woman's. She pointed to her closed mouth and shook her head. And then to her ears. He looked at her as if she'd stood up and pissed over the counter.

Some man'll strike it rich!

He turned his back to her. She sipped her coffee. It was warming and strong and didn't interfere with the drug too much. When the little cup was almost empty she tapped it on the counter. A man with a newspaper had taken a stool, looked her over. The young man behind the counter came over to her. His lips were dry.

You tap like that again, pétasse......

As he leaned in towards her, cigarettes on his breath, his face not at all uninviting yet its expression familiar, she slammed the elegant little cup into the side of his head, the sticky coffee-and-sugar mixture clotting and gluing the shards of white pottery against his skull, a small harmless trickle of blood appearing like a worm from thick black grass. He made a face, almost sexual, like the faces the painter made, and the one the young man had made when she'd swallowed him, she took pleasure in seeing that expression, put his hand to the side of his face and took a step backwards. *Pouffiasse!* The man with the newspaper had a smile on his face.

She was off the stool, running across the platform, feeling her feet slap the polished platform, *pluff-plud-pluff* went her small bag against her side, the official black cleaners in their green uniforms moving around as if the whole world might drop a gigantic cigarette on their polished kingdoms and they'd have to be there when that happened, she pushed and shoved and got outside and no one followed her, no one pursued her, because, of course, she was becoming invisible, it was morning, a hot sunny morning full of glowing taxis and the whole world taking a train and she was a small girl with damp hair, who, quite obviously, was in a panic because she'd missed her train.

Marcel, moving in the gathering glow of a new hot morning; the radio on, he made himself at home here, but was territorial in his own place, and he showering, the water spitting and spatting and slapping, you could hear it all over the room, even as the *avocat* lay there half in and out of sleep, he could hear it, that halfway point between sleeping and waking when everything is still a dream, warm and unthreatening; the splutter of the coffee pot, the warm thick male smell of coffee brewing, he watched the sun flatten great swathes of golden light across the walls, over the bed, blinding and welcoming.

He lifted himself up, smelled Marcel on the single sheet, it was so warm even at night one sheet did the trick, and that other sea-smell, odour of sea-wrack and ammonia, the scent of their lovemaking, warm still on the air of the bed from who knew what hour of the morning and out of what necessity, for he had been tired, oddly bewildered, and discomfited by the presence of that novel.

When he thought of it now, sheet pulled down around his white chest, letting the cooler air of the room dry him, he sweated, his skin was slippery, Marcel had opened a big window, he could hear the street; when he thought of it now it ran around the inside of his skull pursued by a small army of other, more important things that clamoured for his attention; his mother, his Irish client. What must morning be like for him? The melancholy thought was delicious and soothing. He coughed a few times and got out of bed, skinny legs, bony, propping themselves on the floor, the mat, the carpet, fragile and unattractive, what compelled him to think that he had ever been attractive? Perhaps when he'd been younger, a universal truth, when he'd run in that crazy little group about the Sorbonne, willing exiles, glorying in being outcasts, sausage-eaters, cheese-heads, the first time he had kissed another male had been back then, and the others he'd slept with were faces now, some famous enough in a small-beer way to make the papers now and then, and Marcel – the water eased off, Marcel was humming – had arrived like an engine being switched off. As if comfort were come at last! Release from the tedium of having to *find* someone. Marais queens, grown old gracelessly, like grubby pirates daring the risk under the trees, one or two of them, the truckers playing Russian Roulette with rent-boys, flesh on flesh, no condom, the price is higher; *there* was a scene the suicidally lonely could descend to like walking down an endless sloping tunnel into the bowels of an enormous and relentlessly hungry animal.

He sat on the edge of the bed, naked, his penis flaccid and stupid-looking, like a drunk slapped in the face, and he heard Marcel coming out of the bathroom – *what about that novel?* – then, looking up saw him, a snow-white towel wrapped around him, one of *his* best, Marcel playing lewd, *Ooops! I seem to have caught my towel on a nail!*

The sound of the coffee pot grew louder, more jarringly argumentative. On a bedside table – the question was finding the edges of his mouth now – lay three files, elegantly labelled for his attention, his name honoured with the title by which tea-boys and public lower ranks were ordered to address him, *Maître.* From the street came a nervous blaring of horns and a pigeon had found his way uselessly onto the warming window sill. Under his grandiose and dusty title, the arms of Paris, that delicate little sailing boat, a child's plaything: *Fluctuat nec Mergitur.*

Marcel sat beside him and rested his wet Arabesque of a head on his naked, bony shoulder, he felt embarrassed and ashamed of his puniness, his balding head and increasing years – well, they increased no matter what – and Marcel gave a sigh, hot breath searing his wet shoulder, wet from his own sweat, as if Marcel had had something on the edge of his mind about to be born in words, when he said against his own better judgment, *Since when did you start reading African authors?* Feeling Marcel sit away from him suddenly, hearing him say *Oh, now, since when was that a sin? You have always told me reading goes with writing. Are you a literary racist?* The tone of the reply, the whole conversation for that matter, was at too great a variance with the sun on the wall, the hot street outside, the cooing of the singular pigeon. There was a DJ manically happy on the radio.

Of course Marcel was entitled to read whatever he liked, there were some great North African novelists, Camus, for example, it was just that he'd never heard of this particular author so he should calm down, what was he prying for? What heavy stone was he trying to look beneath? Well, perhaps in some arrogant way he believed he had led Marcel, over a great length of time, through all the literary learning he now possessed; his first gift to him had been a poetry book, and this had inspired him – so Marcel often said, anyway – and now his poems were appearing, slowly, slowly, with the great effort of events that have no importance and Marcel was happy; *so, shouldn't I be proud?*

They took their coffee from delicate tiny cups, black and sweetened, nakedly beside one another on the bed hearing the morning rise along the boulevard, it would slip over the tiled elegant roofs and up the faces of the proud ramshackle buildings like a veil lifted from the face of a beautiful sad boy. Over the doors of these heroic edifices the carved bearded faces, the elegant lions, the torsos of mythic heroes, shook themselves and lived in the rays of the rising sun. *You are jealous that I can choose for myself, that I own my tastes in books*, Marcel had said a moment ago. And the *avocat* had daintily, nakedly sipped his coffee, feeling his wet body drying, wondering how in God's name Marcel, whom he knew so well, had come to use a phrase such as *own my tastes*, a ridiculous choice of words, words *that were not his*, the sort of thing you'd find in a self-help or find-your-inner-child piece of shit in the leftover basket of any otherwise decent bookshop. So who or what led him to such phrases? The radio? The TV? Or led him to such a novel, or was he trying to *find himself?* This slender half-Arab, this model of a half-breed *raton* in a city of every race under the sun? Was that really so threatening? An African Apollinaire. The next thing the silly shit would be reading the Koran, there was a weird atmosphere about these days, people were under pressure to know who they really were, or might be.

The *avocat* realised he was letting his imagination and his fears get the better of him. *It is because of that 'phone message about my mother,* he thought. *I am like a lost child in the big city again because of it. What would she say if she could see me, naked, like this?* Marcel pushed him gently over, prompting him in a panic to find a place on the floor for his emptying coffee cup.

"Don't."

But he may just as well have been talking to himself. Marcel had that power over him, purely sexual – he could conquer him in nothing else, least of all the dexterity of his mind – and he used his tongue along his shoulder now, gently down the inside of his arm, then rattling the edges of his ribcage as a child rattles a stick along a set of railings.

"You don't trust me."

"It's not that at all," said the *avocat.*

Well, of course it was that. Their difference in ages, Marcel's craving to be noticed, that dark energy he possessed or which possessed him, which made his body writhe among the café tables all the more for the guiding laser of the eyes of other men on his buttocks, his thighs; how could you ever tell he wasn't flirting, and perhaps flirted all day? A few streets down and there was the Marais and God only knew what he could get up to in there. Or on the steps of the rue des Mauvais Garcons, its population was once so dangerous, God help us, used to be called rue Chartron, thirty-three metres long and a place to be seen, to stop off, politely gay these days, you walked up it from the rue de Rivoli into the Street of The Glass-maker; now Marcel's tongue had moved to the bend in his knee and with exquisite tenderness – how could anyone understand or appreciate how one man could be as tender as this with another? – Marcel stroked the rising waddle of his penis with one long finger.

"It's not that," he heard himself say, lying because that's what such a delicious feeling could make him do. His voice was hoarse, his throat was dry, he needed air but suffocation was all of a sudden infinitely preferable if he were to lose his breath at the touch of Marcel's finger. Marcel moved himself upright, then pushed himself between the *avocat's* legs, doing with his tongue what he had been doing with his finger. *And in the Fourth Arrondissement they could all go and fuck themselves! Drag the bastards out to the Parvis Notre Dame and flay them alive! Chain them in the Conciergerie!*

Marcel's movements marched, strolled, sauntered up to the head of his penis, then floated around its tip. *Washed over but not submerged.*

The *avocat,* knowing he'd be late for the office, late for the whole day, late for the rest of his life, yielded and took Marcel's wiry head in his hands and pushed him down; his penis flicked upwards, elastic and awkward out of Marcel's way and they both had a quick, breathy laugh and there was a terrific outpouring, immense and solid and ugly and over very quickly, the pigeon on the windowsill flapped into the air and some scraps of feathers floated down gently to the floor of the room, gently rocking back and forth, wisps of things.

Marcel got up quickly. The *avocat's* penis stood for a moment and then, like the hand of a soldier who has saluted the wrong officer, dropped quickly. Marcel was at the window where the pigeon had been. There was noise, a variety of noises, in the street. There was a thin sound, like an electric saw moving deep into wood. Marcel was at the window.

"Oh! Oh, Mother!"

And then he bent double and threw up all over the floor.

The *avocat* got off the bed, the scent of his petulant penis cloying and embarrassing now, and waddled towards Marcel. Marcel sat down on the floor and hugged himself. His mouth was wet with the black juice of coffee and he began to shake his head. The carpet was ruined.

The noises in the street grew much louder, yet indistinguishable. Only the high thin screech maintained its command. He looked out and saw a crowd beginning, people rushing, straining to see what had happened, and he saw in the middle of the road a human arm wrapped in a blue cloth, a light thing, what a girl would wear, and there was a lip of blood to it where it had been severed, very neatly, he thought; he felt dizzy but fascinated, not in the least nauseous. He forgot all about Marcel, and also that, if anyone looked over, they'd see a middle-aged, potbellied man standing naked in the open window; out from under a 'bus protruded two naked legs and the back wheel of a push-bike and the thin bladed screeching came from under there somewhere. Suddenly a woman in the gathering crowd fainted and a small mob gathered to attend to her.

Was tragedy a fickle matter of taste? The screeching stopped and there was nothing in the air now, no sound at all. It seemed a very long time before he heard the rhythmic thump of the ambulance siren bulling up the street. In the meantime Marcel had taken another shower.

The *avocat* had closed the big window and realised that he was now quite late indeed. He had dressed himself and used an electric shaver. He had sprayed some *Hysope* eau-de-toilette around his cheeks and neck: he had been conscious all the time of the sounds beyond the window, however muted they might be now they were still insistent, the gabbling of voices, the opening and closing of officious-sounding doors, this sort of thing; he knew it all without looking at it, the sort of thing he could conjure up in a courtroom – the polished hush and crusty fragrance of the Palais de Justice and the sound of expensive shoes creaking down the long halls, intoxicating to a *flaubertois* – make people see without seeing, hear without hearing, that was part of his job. So what use was this other reality? They would wash away the blood and take away the severed arm – he had no doubt that the end of the screeching had marked the end of a woman's life, old or young. Perhaps not, of course, perhaps she'd just passed out.

There were still people standing about – a riddle of blood, not much, striped the road and, of course, police were measuring this distance and that and interviewing a trembling 'bus-driver who sat with his head in his hands half in and half out the door of a police car, and all the passengers had been asked to leave the 'bus and some stood around appalled and others were just annoyed to be kept late by some silly woman cycling under a 'bus; but he had closed the big door behind him, Marcel still in the shower and he gave himself, for form's sake, a few moments to look and frown and stare, and then all anyone would have seen was this dapper yet casually-dressed, important-looking man with a thin designer briefcase making his way briskly to the end of the street where the taxis waited.

There were church bells clanging in the distant air when he woke up; perhaps they had roused him, he slept very lightly, a mere drowse, and only for an hour or so at a time.

He'd had to emerge, gasping like a drowning man breaking the surface of a stream in flood, from a dream of the painter and the painter's chaotic studio. And when he opened his eyes the dream and its memory faded quickly.

A light sweat had developed along the collar of his vest. The air in the cell was hot and thick with the stench of the squat. Panic fluttered his heart, the same way love might. Then it subsided.

When he thought about the condom over the door he was filled with a momentary brutality, a desire to kill and hurt which flared like a lighted match in a dark room and as quickly went out again. When the anger subsided, a small worm of self-pity inserted itself at the base of his throat and wriggled there. Pictures entered his head then, trailing like some sort of mad banner across the bone-yellow screen of his skull.

A routine, dull and alarming, sometimes illuminating, had built itself around him; the painter offering him decent conversation and now and then there were gatherings in the studio, hardly meriting to be called parties, drunken, dope-addled and noisy, a wonder indeed the neighbours – mostly elderly men and women who dressed smartly and moved with incredible slowness down the street, he saw them every day – didn't complain. The painter would create an elegant fuss: *Move that there! Give me a hand with this! You don't want someone sitting on next month's rent!* This last remark a joke, because the painter had done well enough for himself, his stubbornly quaint paintings – those *faux*-Arcadian landscapes in the background, turrets, shepherds with sticks, rivers that merged with the sky, windmills – seemed to sell; the mock-confusion and panic around getting the studio into some kind of order was like the paintings themselves, an attractive fakery, a show reminiscent of an earlier time when this sort-of Jewish painter who died his hair red had order of a sort in his life, and it gave them all something to do.

The girl was commanded to buy a variety of small eatables, crackers, decent cheese, and the painter would hand her a list and lean over her and instruct her directly into her face so that she would not mistake a word and could read his lips clearly. The wine he would go out for himself, a conceit of dreadful innocence, for he would go no farther than the gaudy and inexpensive Arab shop on the corner, bark in his Cockney-salted but precise French and buy the cheapest wine, usually North African, on the shelf. And plenty of cigarettes, sometimes an entire carton. Under a bomb-site of books and newspapers lay the paint-splattered CD player, it was a marvel that it worked at all, and he would dig out something Jazzy, Bluesy, a compilation, he was fond of Dinah Washington, and as the frenzied excavations in his studio carried on – a Paris businessman painted against a mediaeval castle wall, a young girl, nude, emerging on a conch-shell from the sea, the owner of the Arab shop dressed as a friar in a cowl – all these visual miracles rocking and submerging one through and under the other all over the place – there was Dinah singing *Blues for a Day* or *All or*

Nothing, a world beneath the paintings, the this-and-thatness of the room gradually emerging, chairs, a respectable if ruined settee, you saw them for a day or two at a time and then they'd sink under the deluge again, he kept a pile of very old copies of *Playboy* tied gracefully with a red ribbon beneath a tottery Pisan Tower of shattered suitcases in a corner and the suitcases concealed sinister holes in the skirting, at night a pianoforte of scratchings and graspings, you learned to live with it because the room had a strange coziness to it, it was a haven with its own stretch of ancient cobbled yard, and the high buildings surrounding it gave an oddly romantic feel to the place, as if you could look up through the one dirty window of this studio and see turrets and drawbridges and towers anytime you liked, the magic was there if you knew where and how, perhaps, to look, a circle protecting them etched in the flagstones.

The painter was by no means a bad cook and the three-ringed electric cooker was the only area of the room he kept constantly accessible – the room did not possess a sink or running water, the lavatory was across the yard and his own upstairs room had the decent bathroom. Fat pots emerged, half-cleaned from their last use and in these he would produce a stew of some sort, or now and then a practical curry and even more delicate delights, such as a *salade de haricots blancs*, or a *salade de pissenlits*, this last with a great runny egg in it, balsamic vinegar in a crusty bottle, a pepper-mill of acute refinement, made of carved wood, a cookery book of withered pages seared with pencil jottings, a virtual palimpsest, resting against the flaking wall like an old man out of breath; but these dishes were only for occasions when one or two special guests, mostly painters or the owner of a gallery, were invited, and they seemed either to be at home in or openly delight in his clutter. Baguettes were purchased, and paper plates; the proprietor of the Arab shop would grin and joke with him that he was entertaining a woman. And great plastic bottles of Evian or something similar and on occasion a pack of inexpensive beer. He would whistle to the music as he worked, refusing all access to where he did his chopping and dicing, throw himself into the cooking, a suddenly fragile and rather sad red-capped figure hunched in a corner, his hands and upper arms jerking furiously, his big made-up head keeping time; you could watch him and feel a mysterious and often brutal melancholy rising like bile in your throat, he distanced you and went into the distance himself, you became his children, he was showing off to you, *Look how civilised and practical I can be, you're safe here with the Yid;* and all you felt was this sadness which was about him at first and then became about you, and you grabbed some more cheap red Maghrebi wine to drown the longing for what that swept over you, a knowledge of your own incompleteness, and when the girl offered you a joint you did not hold back, the smell mixing with the exotic balsams, the peppers, the painter not looking over his shoulder and just saying *Don't start that shit early, you'll get stoned and you won't eat what I'm making here,* which made you feel even worse.

They'd arrive eventually, the sun still hot in the yard, a dangerous table set up and a few chairs, they'd eat outside, real Bohemians, the smell of paint and thinners and reefer and cheap cigarettes and some not so cheap, and the painter would put on a decent and gaudy shirt, usually short-sleeved and make remarks loudly on the fusty air – cats crawled cautiously along the shards of the mediaeval walls, you could hear an old man clearing his throat somewhere up in the sky in an apartment, perhaps the one with the window always open – and he'd make jokes about a wife he never otherwise referred to, mentioned, even suggested, who was either dead or dissolved into the world in some obscure way, and he would skip from reasoned French to street-English depending on the company – though he'd only seen one native of France, husband to a nervous, anorexic Californian woman who'd once been very pretty and now looked wrecked but dressed in gauzy, suggestively transparent dresses, bare legs and expensive-looking sandals, her skin wet and melty-buttery in appearance, she was always drunk, the painter winked at her and joked with her as if, not long ago, he'd had her and needed to remind her – doing things fussily like a house-proud wife, pouring everyone drinks, issuing orders to bring this and fill that, the girl stupidly full of *ganj* and red wine, her lips light purple, slopping things around, suddenly the flagstones and cobbles of the yard were sprinkled with green leaves or shards of meat or drips of vinegar or snows of salt and at night the rats would clean it all up and the cats would eat the rats; they were a motley company, middle-aged, elegant and restless, feigning – as the paintings feigned – a different time in their heads, becoming sixteen and fancy-free again, or thinking they could, the Americans the most predictable, heads full of Hemingway and what they'd read of Paris, divorces behind them like vehicles in a pile-up, writing the novel they'd meant to write when they were twenty, here a dozen years and not a decent phrase of French, didn't need it, all their friends spoke English, they spoke of *upgrading* their apartment or the entire world; even the solitary Frenchman didn't speak French at these gatherings for fear of appearing foreign but struggled through English like a swimmer suddenly finding dangerous rocks in a familiar river; there was also a rigidly tall Englishman who'd once been a barrister but was now a sculptor, who boasted loudly about how Kenzo in the Place des Victoires had taken one of his works – *a representational nude man,* he described it with hungry flourishes of his skeletal hands – to use in a display of their Summer Collection; there was an Irish woman, in her forties and wearing too much make-up, around whose attractive shoulders the painter now and then draped himself, introduced her, *You must have something to discuss,* winking at him, but they had nothing to discuss, the woman smelled of something leaking and was ferociously shy and hadn't been in Ireland for a quarter of a century, she wrote articles on French art for a prominent Irish art journal and was divorced from a French husband and her children were dying at La Sorbonne, they were lucky, she was lucky, she loved Paris and was writing a critical study of Montaigne, this literary direction was new and exciting for her; and at the end of the evening, inevitably, she would weep quietly to herself and the painter would call her a taxi; hysterical people, from everywhere and nowhere, writing scraps of poetry, short stories, or a novel, or painting something, sculpting something, the majority in their spare time, living on a mysterious and perhaps shared fund of money or working at something they hated – they'd profess their hatred openly and there was always running beneath their ordinary complaint a current of something more vicious – and they loved Paris and loathed it and all France with theatrical passion, at the criticism stage they did not spare themselves in front of a French guest: the Parisians were rude, after twenty years among them you got to *know* this, they were often dirty – well, you can *tell* – and the food was terrible; or the Parisians were wonderful, the women so elegant, the styles, the different *skin*-tones, from a sort of yellow to a not-quite-black, the things you could buy here for relatively nothing, *but those bloody locks on their windows*; America's fucked, Bush has got us hated all over the world, I'd never go back, France has flair, a sense of itself, or do you say *her*self? an identity, good luck to them for telling us to bugger off, why should the French fight for George W. Bush, tell me that? Britain made a mistake, Enoch Powell was right all those years ago, *rivers of blood*, I still have a problem here with all the Africans, and you tell me the French aren't racist, I can tell you they *are*, whole areas of this city I just won't *go*, it's like being, I don't know, name some place in Africa, it's like being *there* and maybe I sound bad but if I want to live among Arabs I'll go there, to an Arab country, that fanaticism, it comes from the mosques, who the fuck believes in God anyway anymore? My grandfather used to say *Castrate them all at Calais!* But there's no Britain left that I'd want anything to do with. You walk into the bloody Tower of London now there's an Indonesian as a tour guide! I've got a nice French woman who oils my dick and isn't high maintenance and she doesn't nag me like an Englishwoman would. Let's not knock the French – a deprecating glance in the direction of the murderously smiling French husband – because that sort of criticism is merely a form of envy, at least that's what I'm hearing over here and fuck politics, the French know how to live, I say. London's a dive these days, I was there last summer, my daughter asked me over, I shouldn't have gone. I'm not a bangers-and-mash man anymore, thank God. I've gotten used to the good life. Look, see this hat? If I wore this in London they'd call me a *fag!* Or this shirt, for God's sake. Got it in a sale. What's that funny French word? *Solde.* That's it. Sold. No, it's more *sauled.* I'd love to learn French, really I would, but if I took time to do that I'd never get anything done. My husband is learning English. His English is *excellent,* he has nothing to learn! *Thang 'u.* Regarding the shirt and that wide hat – *are* you a fag? Ha-ha! Fuck you! Let's go to the boulevard Bessières and I'll prove I'm not with a dainty little Ukrainian lass! Hey! Here's a good one! Why do women get thrush? *So they can learn how to deal with an irritating cunt in case they marry one!* Now come on, ladies, don't pretend you're embarrassed, women always tell the filthiest jokes. Dinah Washington – and someone drops a glass and it shatters and there's a bit of swearing and the chatter resumes.

Wine-stains on the cobbles and the flagstones, bloody flecks, explosions, like TV pictures of a 'bus-stop after a suicide-bombing, darkening; bits of food scattered here and there, the light dimming, the air very warm, over the wall the occasional drifting sounds of the outside world, the pumping skirl of a police-car, someone's laughter. The painter watching the scene from a corner, taking a moment or two out of the fray, designing his next move – always a trickle of panic on his face – and the direction things would take, moving forward with a smile as wide as his widest canvas:

"I love you people! *Arbeit macht frei!* I say nuke the whole bloody lot of 'em, get the dogs, you're all a bunch of bloody Nazis! More drink all round, bring back the rack! Here, your glass's empty."

And they'd laugh *hah-hah!* A sad dig against some teensy-weensy part of himself, that's what the wine did or perhaps it was what he thought he had to do, it was bad to hear anyway. And the conversation, darkly defused, would move politely, after an embarrassed moment or two for breath, into a discussion of something brazenly useless and just for him, he looked like a real Jew in those moments waiting for one of his guests to 'phone for the men in hats and black leather coats, his bags packed, you pitied him and the wine and whatever else exaggerated everything, you wanted to stand up for him, throw the whole lot of them out, they were a lost bunch anyway; the girl, grown cheaply beautiful, would be sitting down now, one leg over the other, a dress on for the occasion, sipping as delicately as any debutante, thinking her own thoughts and more than once she'd stand up violently, everyone would look round at her and the look on her face said *If I could speak I would scream.* The painter would try to keep the gatherings light and warm but they always overcooked, always ended up burned around the edges, he recognised himself in his guests, swallowed gobfuls of wine to dull the sensation, at least that's what you began to think, for he became increasingly edgy as the evening went on, no longer bothering with frantic energy to put on a new CD, not caring whether someone's glass was full or empty, the light gone in the little courtyard, a blue night coming on full of hesitant stars and a 'plane going over, its red wing lights twinkling, he couldn't play host anymore and something seemed to weigh him down, the energy going out of his guests too, one by one they'd flutter away and merge with the falling night, the taxi for the sad Irish woman arrived and gone.

They'd sit, the painter, himself, the girl, in a blessed twilight silence, the air warm and quiet, sipping the last wine, surveying the littered yard, someone would produce a spliff; whatever the evening had been was gone long ago.

Then the painter would snuggle beside the girl, curiously fatherly, and she would put an arm around his bent shoulder. Eventually he would throw a glass hard against a dark wall, then another, then yet another, until the girl took his big ageing head in his hands and caressed it; he would look at the two of them, the vignette they made, the almost-holiness about it, that intimate silence, only, if he listened carefully, the sound of the girl's hands sifting through the man's hair, at this point they had merged, become one in the darkness, and he was alone again, cast out, or so he felt. He would stand up, make for the studio. The painter would say something, mutter something he could not interpret, or simply emit, from the depth of the girl's arms, a loud and long growl.

He would go into the studio – the smells of cooking were now the scents of a deep nostalgia, like dead flowers in a graveyard – and settle himself on the settee, listen for a while to the painter muttering to a girl who could not hear him and who, in the dark, could not read his lips.

He would fall asleep, hoping never to wake up.

In front of her now an enormous green phallus, fat and ornate, reared up with a man's face wrapped around it. A bearded face, kindly and strong, on its brow the words 'Phillippe Noiret', and on a grizzled cheek, two others, 'Victor Hugo'.

As she went nearer the *colonne Morris* seemed to inflate until its glistening greeny mushroom head was many feet above her; she reached out and touched it, felt the reassuring cold of old iron and the Perspex of the big advertising hoarding, her fingers lingering on the painted elderly ornament. Noiret seemed to be wearing a jolly velvety hat. A fat woman pushed a buggy past her and the child and the woman looked at her, no more than a glance, and then they were gone. She rested her cheek against the great French actor's and felt the yielding cool of the plastic. She was on a corner, and all around her big yellow apartments with their perfect black wrought-iron railings seemed to form an unassailable cliff; she was at the bottom of a ravine. She pushed herself off the advertisement and walked quickly across the street.

On an island in the middle of the road was an old and locked carousel, the paint peeling, the blue and green and red prancing horses looking tired and sad, their little painted heads bowed under the big galley-chains. She wanted to sit up on one of them, feel the hard childhood wood beneath her, a strange and rushing urge, filling the vacuum in her belly where a moment before a coming-down anxiety had unhinged the world.

There were scenes painted around the carousel's hat, streets in a city she vaguely recognised, women in long skirts and men with walking-canes. She felt that if she could only reach out and touch the pictures, she would at once be swallowed into their comfort and distance. Suddenly, she felt very tired. She walked on, startled for a moment by the slow menace of a police-car driving by, but it moved away from her, dragged into the city on an invisible wire, a child's toy. She felt the playful weight of the carousel fall away behind her, like a shirt falling off your shoulders because it no longer fitted you. On a lamppost in front of her now, another face, a young man, cropped hair, scowling, the paper around him, framing him, falling off in shards and tatters as if he had already been forgotten. She read:

'Carlo GIULIANI – 23 ans, assassiné le Vendredi 20 juillet 2001 à Genes par l'armée italienne gardienne de l'ordre des chefs d'état et de gouvernement des pays les plus riches, le G8.'

She stroked the young shaved face, the open throat, and read the words over and over, not grasping their significance, saddened – her emotions were all over the place, she knew that would happen, tired as she was, and coming down, but nonetheless it was unpleasant – by the raggy poster, and she wondered if memory were like that, a tattering of images until at last there was nothing remaining and the heart was a blank sheet again.

She moved on. The city, this morning, seemed full of faces which she needed to touch; but she touched only their illusive representations, what someone had designed or reproduced; the painter, leaning over his canvas, looking at her, saying, *Here! See what I've done with you! I've made you into a duchess! A dirty duchess, that's you. Look! See what I've done with your eyes!* And she'd waver up and walk over to him, sensing his almost sexual excitement – the young man was gone out somewhere, it didn't matter where, maybe to the dilapidated café where the painter'd cajoled a job for him a couple of days a week dragging beer barrels around, washing glasses, but she could feel herself with the painter without any ambivalence – and she'd smell his fatherly lover's sweat and paint, and resting her hand on his shoulder, the hairs on his chest like silver wires curled and springy, and she'd peer at what representation he'd made of her, a cowled head, the background of leaping mythical animals, a unicorn perched in the distance over her right shoulder, what was she to make of all that? Castles, turrets, the sky a murderous blue. It was her image alright, the eyes, he'd caught them very well so that the painting was more of a mirror than a painting, she looked at herself looking back out at herself from another world. The painter's lips were moving but he wasn't facing her so she couldn't make out what he said; perhaps he spoke only to himself, absorbed in what he did, and she could look at his brush and imagine, no, *hear*, the bristles gorged with paint moving like a whisper over her cheeks and lips. It was an odd, unmusical sound, flat and monotonous, a single note, perhaps, a *shuss-suss-sussh.* When he lifted the tip of his brush from the canvas the sound stopped. And still she could hear nothing else. Whatever mocking miracle occurred was part of the brush and the canvas, not of the world around it or beyond it or separate from it.

She watched him paint again, and again that oddly hopeful whispering sound, and saw that he omitted the yellowing bruise, the size of a small coin, just under her chin where he'd struck her, she couldn't remember why and it scarcely mattered, but it had made the young man very angry and he'd taken her by the shoulders and yelled at her – at least his mouth was open wide and his face grimaced which, sexually, was a yell, so perhaps all yelling was sexual – and she'd felt the cold pricks of his spittle on her face. *Look what I've made of your face!* the painter said, excited.

Now she found herself before a pastry shop, the inside a huddle of well-dressed grandmotherly women chattering loudly – how rapidly their mouths moved, those fluttering wing-like lips, some dry and others moist, moving as if they existed by themselves – confident in their good make-up and expensive scarves. She found herself looking at them over the shelves of marvellous cakes, wondrous pastries, ingenious meringues, miraculous breads gleaming with shivers of icing, honey glazing; so much cream, thick and luxurious and faintly exciting, and the blood-red sheen of cherries and the melting glacier-slow movement of layers of chocolate; the open grain of brown bread, tiny spills of grain and shards of crust on the immaculate white paper mats, their edges frilled like a child's First Communion dress; round and intricate designs and patterns of bread, *brioches*, and thick and slim rolls, *baguettes* and *pains, tartes aux pommes* with their lightly layered swirls of apple-slices and a dusting of white icing-sugar, jars of honey, jars of jam: the women chattered on, frowning, bantering, arguing, adjusting themselves, tightening those expensive scarves. She went inside and the working mouths stopped. Suddenly the women seemed more intent upon buying whatever it was they'd come in to buy; she'd reminded them of something, or perhaps threatened their positions near the counter. As she pressed behind them she took into her nostrils the sharp spice of herself drifting lazily up from between her legs, a feather's weight of menstrual blood, the sea-deep bitterness of her womb, and then it was gone.

In the street again she chewed deeply, gratefully, on a small cherry tart dressed in paper flounces, crumbs falling the thousand feet or more from her mouth to the pavement, her lips sticky with the honey, the sweet cream, seeds ticking at the edges of her teeth. The quick rush of sugar made her feel better. She took a moment now to inspect herself in a shop window, saw her face, a brittle attractiveness under a honey-glaze of sleep. She could not keep wearing the same clothes, they'd smell, they'd scream of the streets. She needed something to quell the salty tang of her womanness; she found that too, and was proud of the well-designed little shopping-bag into which it was dropped by a girl of rugged, dark beauty, just enough make-up carefully applied to the eyelashes, the lips, no need for anything on the facial skin save a light powdering to keep down the natural dark sheen in case it became too much and began to look like sweat or dampness; the girl in a snow-white overall and a badge announcing her name and her in a tight curled crop, one side browny-red and the other coal-black. She saw the word on the girl's badge: *Nezhia.* How understanding Nezhia had been, how quick to realise that she could neither hear nor speak, how being women with a small ordinary woman's problem made language redundant! They could be great friends, Nezhia could invite her back to her house, they'd eat together, she'd become part of the family......

But the painter would not be able to find her.

She had pictures in her head again – faces, faces – and her heart worked hard, hard, against the perilously thin wall of her bone and skin. Why didn't it just burst and have done with it! She needed something, and for a time she simply took stock of where she was, where she'd walked to, how far from here or there, she opened up a secret box in her head that contained all the information, the maps, the codes, that anyone would need to live on the streets of Paris.

She was standing in front of a yellowing wall, now, which was pocked by bullet-marks, and it looked like the face of a dealer she'd known who'd give small scores out for a fuck, but the Mur des Fédéres was where revolutionaries had died, that much she knew, and she moved away quickly from it. The cartwheel iron grilles around the bottoms of the trees gleamed and shimmered in the low persistent heat, a woman with a shaved head walked a small black dog on an extending lead. She looked up and saw a sky as deeply and upsettingly blue over avenue Gambetta as a child's crying eyes. She felt timid and fragile, a bad way to feel. As if she were ill. A filthy removal van passed her by in a burst of smoke; snaking across its broad rear doors, in red paint sprayed in a clumsy, hasty hand, the single word *fuijs*.

She turned a corner in her retreat into boulevard de Ménilmont, walked, slowing down, until she came to a wide entrance and went in: and sprawled before her like a child's house of bricks all tumbled down, so many shapes and angles, gods, devils, cones, slabs, flowers, cherubim and seraphim and musical instruments and instruments of war and scrolls and crosses and names, so many names frozen in stone and marble forever lay crawling upwards towards the beckoning cold last homes of Haussmann, Musset, Colette, Rossini, whose grave-doors she would pass before any others; their silent presence no more or less soundless to her than anything else in the world; this welcoming dead city of *Père* Lachaise.

The *avocat* took himself off to try to read his book as far as the Place des Vosges and was content, for a short while to sit on a bench in mannerly disorder, filled roll lying here, a black coffee there, and watch innumerable young mothers playing with their children, gossiping animatedly, exposing their limbs to the squared hot sun, poised like mannequins in a painter's tableau on the cropped flat green grass. He had spent the morning preparing to interview the Irishman and trying to erase the groove in his head of a scream from beneath a 'bus; he'd told them in the office, and had received the usual gasps – which meant, and indicated, neither concern nor reflection – and by the water-cooler, addressed as *Maître*, he had received into his hand like a blessed wafer the file once again on the urgent matter of his Irish client.

Police, he was informed, had so far been unsuccessful in finding the girl or anyone answering to her description, though there had been an interesting incident in a train station, they'd been called, a young barman had been injured, he'd given a vague description. Of course *vague*, because no doubt the barman had tried it on.

He glanced up at the ornate buildings around the square, oppressed by their effusive elegance, thought of something he'd read about Madame de Sévigné – an accomplished and cherished gossip in an age when such was prized as a mark of good breeding – and in the distance, he could see a theatrical tailcoat or two, some young people in a quartet playing elegant music between the ornate arches, the chattering tables, the galleries of expensive paintings and sculptures and the shops where prints and postcards were sold; a trace of something languorous by Mozart, a gaggle of tourists with cameras slung on their shoulders, hauling bored teenagers after them like thin petulant dogs on leads.

The city had disappeared. The boisterous restaurants and their no-nonsense waiters in the Place des Vosges were to be avoided at all costs, because without a doubt in the world, he would meet someone there whom he'd know and would know him and his depressing case would come up, the smell of the interview room burst briefly in his nostrils. He planned to examine one or two of the galleries before his lunch break was up and he'd then take a taxi, whatever battling it took on the boiling rue St-Antoine, yet thank God he had long ago made his decision not to drive in Paris in his own car, but the machine badly needed exercise.......

"Hervé! I thought I saw you come in!"

Without being asked, all that loud showiness, the big man made to sit down and the *avocat*, with a housewife's deliberate bustling, put away his book and rearranged his lunch. No, the annoying, prying world had found him out.

"Herbuterne. I was just having a quick lunch."

A private lunch, Herbuterne. But here you are. Overweight, balloon-faced, prosperous, invasive, a cliché of your profession. There is no imagination left in nature. With a familiar feeling of disgust, the *avocat* felt the big man's weight attain the ancient bench and smelled almost at once the lack of success in his deodorant and grisly aftershave. His cheeks were polished veiny red marble, glowing with pumped hot blood and sweat. His shirt was tight and he'd opened, beneath the exasperating spotted tie, the button of the collar. Wiry grey hairs peeped out. He wore an enormous leather jacket, an attempt, perhaps, to drown out the clamour of advancing age, but it made him look like a wealthy pimp. He'd been a sick man for a long time, the liver, he looked unwell in recovery. He had aged.

"Christ, but that roll looks appetising. Me, I'm on a diet. My *third* attempt. Doctors' orders. I take these."

He opened his hand and swallowed, without anything to wash them down, two orange pills. For an absurd moment the *avocat* thought Herbuterne had sought him out as a witness, so that the world would know he'd taken his medication. It was an oddly intimate gesture which unsettled the *avocat*. Theatrical.

The big man looked at him and smiled. The *avocat* took a bite out of his roll, awkwardly, so that he had to fight not to look ugly with pieces of ham and tomato hanging out of his mouth. Embarrassed, he couldn't look up. Chewing, he said quickly:

"You're wasting your time."

Herbuterne feigned hurt. The large flushed face might have been made up, the curtain on a Feydeau farce about to rise. The *avocat* and Herbuterne had long ago spent a drunken night watching the trial of Ceaucescu and his wife, not much of a trial by any decent standards, the *avocat* had noted, a revolutionary trial, necessarily brutal; the old man who could have been any immigrant grandfather reaching across to take his wife's hand, reassure her, even as the generals greased their guns, the spurts of yellow dust in the café TV, the sound only a *mitraillette* can make, the old man had fallen backwards, his legs awkwardly beneath him in shiny blue trousers, two peasants in the dry dust beneath a blood-blotched wall, it was all quite sad. They had raised their glasses to the Roumanian revolution, yet the *avocat* had not forgotten his feelings of pity and sadness.

From the top pocket of Herbuterne's ungracious leather pimp's jacket a shiny cassette-recorder looked out. To his shame and amusement, the *avocat* thought of the cyclopean head of Marcel's penis.

"Hervé! How long have we known each other?"

No, not a pimp, perhaps, a taxi-driver or a Montparnasse fixer, a man who could get things, arrange things. Herbuterne hung around legal offices waiting for the lost, mislaid word, the hint, the gesture from which a great number of misleading but entertaining paragraphs could be conjured, a magician with words, a professional liar. He was effusively despised, the *avocat* understood that he could not be seen with this man, but he liked some element of him all the same, the nose he had, the ability to know that secrets were, in the end, intolerable. Just as the justice system knew that secrets were the grease in society's wheels; the *avocat* looked over the man's shoulders, a digger like himself, the two of them comrades in arms, one might have said, being generous, and he opened himself to a weary smile.

"I can't imagine how you found me, unless you trailed me here, which is possible."

"You're *news*, Hervé, you're going to have to live with it."

"Is that thing switched on?"

"What! *This?* Of course not."

"I can't help you."

"You have in the past, *Maître.*"

The man's tone grew fat and distasteful. Yes, there had been regrettable occasions when a few harmless morsels, insider gossip, nothing you could be hanged for, still....

"Fuck you, Herbuterne."

The man looked around at nothing in particular. Water fell somewhere, a girl's laughter, a child crying, small rat-like birds scuttling over the listless grass. The air was thick and hot and here and there otherwise staid men drank gulpingly from plastic litre bottles of water. Herbuterne looked about ready to collapse, a heart case in the middle of the friendly disregard of the Place des Vosges. The *avocat* imagined wickedly that he would in such circumstances merely stroll away. He felt wearily compassionate towards the gasping journalist; how humiliating, always to haunt those pristine corridors with their flapping bats of lawyers and judges, waiting to take auguries from their precious droppings. Glutinous thank-yous on venerable uncaring stone stairways.

"A word here, a sip at the tit there. A man's name in the paper has never done him any harm in your profession. The second oldest, I understand. I hear the Irish have sent someone."

"That would be normal procedure."

"Was he fucking her?"

Ah, well, now, there were some details too.... even if there were grains of truth, whole wheatfields of truth; there was a time, always a time, a moment, to turn such as Herbuterne off. Better sooner in this case than later. The whole of Paris suspected – did the whole of Paris, or even one tiny morsel of it, actually care? – that, well, an elderly man, a young man, a pretty girl, however irrational she may be, but the *avocat* was frying another fish, and he had its delicious odours in his nostrils, and for his nostrils only.

The *avocat* stood up, brushed himself down. Pigeons moved in, brazen, cocky. There was an odour of the man that rose as the *avocat* stood up, musky, like the after-smell of sex in a cheap room.

"Word is she was street trash, peddled her ass for a score. Hah! Maybe's she's got a dose, Hervé. Maybe your *Irishman* has. Accident my arse! She was doing the old man, that's for sure."

"Oh, what...."

Those little baits, hooked, barbed; what a good lawyer Herbuterne would have made, in another life. Yes, he'd seen his work. Was the old man living out a hallucinated concoction of fame and young love? What man didn't mourn for the death of possibility? Who bought his paintings now? They'd once been sought after, but the painter's downhill slide was not on trial. A dream, a fantasy, nimbly executed, shadows of past possibility – the sadness of being buried out of sight of your potential, nothing could reach you, yet you went on, surviving – into which he squeezed elements of the real world but not enough of them. *But I am no art critic. Marcel's the artistic one.*

Standing straight now – something had made him, for a moment, feel superior – the *avocat* looked down on the big man. He saw how Herbuterne was losing his hair, how he puffed, making an effort to hide his effort, as he shifted on the bench. How the next liver complaint or heart attack would unsurprisingly kill him.

The *avocat* thought of his mother. He would drive out there, to a room in which no one spoke because no one could hear anything and anyway there was nothing left to hear.

"How am I *news?* What makes this case *news?* Murders happen in this city every day, every hour."

Herbuterne looked up at him as if he were a complete idiot.

"It's a novel, the whole business. Pure Balzac, or perhaps more correctly, Maupassant; talking to fucking daffodils! Madness, mayhem! Who cares? Your Irishman hanged himself with his crap alibis. I'll do a film-script on this before I'm through."

The *avocat* felt ashamed. He couldn't tell whether Herbuterne was serious. Trying to lighten things, he said:

"Well, good luck to you. All I can say, *mon brave,* is that it was a beautiful day until you came along. Goodbye, and don't follow me."

"I'm joking, asshole. Or maybe I'm not. You think I'm the only one you'll have to deal with, *Maître?* Some others, well...."

"He didn't do it."

The words left his mouth like giddy schoolchildren rushing out of school for a summer holiday. Herbuterne looked at him and nodded very slowly as if he understood how much the *avocat* had needed to say what he'd said but he couldn't look at the *avocat* and say *I redeem you*, he wasn't a bloody priest, but the phrase was merely a door against which he had been invited to push, gently, not disturbing anything. He struggled up, his breath coming in leaps, perhaps his throat hurt. He waddled like a nightmare towards the *avocat.*

"You had to get that piece of fuck-all off your chest."

"I suppose so."

"You're his man, you'd be expected to say something like that, even if it's most likely true. Which makes it, by the way, not worth a line of type. Give me more."

"We'll find the girl. *Why am I telling you this?*"

The fat round figure in front of him curtained out so much of the grass, the music, the youthfulness, the peace and escape of the place. It was dead now. Time to go. Herbuterne spoke low now, as if passing long-held secrets, or website addresses where illegal pornography could be found.

"The girl, she's the key? Did your client think they'd believe him? This is France. You're not a bad man, Hervé, and neither am I. I get one more bang in my heart or shiver in the liver working for that rag and that's me. The truth is, I come here frequently enough just to get away. I wish I was divorced, had no children to think about, and was getting fucked by an eighteen-year-old. I saw you completely by accident."

"Your lucky day, then. I said nothing to you, remember that."

"I could cross what's left of my heart and swear to it. Anyway, half Paris is looking for her. They'll find her with a needle in her arm, incoherent. You look worn out. How's Marcel?"

"I think he's having an affair."

"I'm sorry. I wish my wife would have an affair. With *me.*"

The fat big man and the rather prim smaller one stood side by side like mourners at a funeral, at that graveside point where there is a dreadful desire to giggle or laugh outright. They were under the entrance arch now, and behind the *avocat* the heavy roar of rue St-Antoine was like a tide coming in and going out, pregnant with shipwrecks.

"Okay. You've told me nothing, shit-head. For my money it was a three-way fuck that went wrong and the bigger cock got jealous. For everyone's money, come to that. Including the court."

"You are a true Flaubert, Herbuterne. "

Herbuterne's breath smelled of bad teeth and cigarettes. Were they suddenly old friends now?

"Hervé! Don't forget me."

The *avocat* walked off, the heavy slap of Herbuterne's fat hand still on his shoulder, warm, like a splash of sun. It was very hot, he threw away the remains of his roll and coffee. He wanted to weep openly, in the street, like a lost child.

A nervous expectancy washed over him, knowing the lawyer would shortly be sitting in front of him, across a grey scraped and marked table as big and disinterested as a battlefield; he tried to convince himself that these meetings were ultimately useless. At the same time, the lawyer bent the day for him.

He had become neurotically aware of his own being; as if he could count the pores on the skin of his face, or the hairs on his own head. He could look in the polished steel square that passed for a mirror on his wall and see every small red canal and vein in his eyes, almost see the minute and regular pulsings of blood through those perilous channels. On the backs of his hands he saw freckles, or the beginnings of cancers, he had not noticed before, and his heart pounded at the thought of his own death. He saw that the meagre paint on the walls of his cell flaked in generous, map-shaped portions, as if previous prisoners – and what a terrifying and doomed word that was – had attempted to recreate the continents of anxiety and guilt and hope through which their waking dreams propelled them.

And perhaps for some those voyages had ended only when the head had been separated from the body, which was nothing but unthinking meat without it.

With great difficulty he woke, even if he managed to sleep, of which he could never be certain, to a trembling in the walls of the cell which may have been an echo of the tremblings of his own soul; he saw too often the painter's generous face and heard his enchanting lies told as a grandfather tells tales to his children's children; of a life impossible in London as it would have been impossible anywhere in the known world, so exotic and criminal, the animals haunting its Bohemian jungles beyond any human redemption except, so the painter held, through the almost religious intensity of their art and the sobering power of drink. Bacon flagellated the canvas and his lovers were never any match for the gross necessity of his being; he was an ikon to the doomed poets of the homosexual illicit nightmare of the times. Oh, yes, once the painter – it was great to be so young in those days! - had been back to that notorious blitzkrieged studio and had disturbed someone on a couch and then there were things done with whips, you wouldn't believe, and he wasn't the only one, why settle for him? He's the one we all know. Irish, too, like you. Though he never played that card. Unlike Brendan Behan, an insufferable drunk, who played the Paddy to the last, parodied himself, was avoided in most watering-holes even by his own kind, he came in one door, you went out the other, my son, if you had sense. Made much of his stay in Paris if he thought you were interested, but it was a drunken rout. Wrote porn.

Memories as unfinished canvases, sketches on wormy wood. Was what he painted simply the dreamlike ancientness of his London past? The men looked handsome but debauched and the women looked like boys or whores. *Could've had a rockstar, well, we later even moved in the same circles as Jagger and Marianne, she was a beauty, wanted to marry me.* Famous, half-remembered names dropped like stones into the well of achievement, a deep and bottomless hole if ever there was one. And that dreadful hint of intimacy.

The stories went on and on, sometimes hash-spiced, or the girl had obtained something else, or there was a good bottle of something lying about, he even had a bottle of genuine Russian vodka, with Stalin's face on the label. Into the Paris night, a cosiness, a warmth worth holding onto, just the three of them, the bruise on her cheek or arm almost faded, like a shadow on a diseased lung which gradually responds to treatment. *Did you know it was always said that my uncle painted, or at least drew things, in Treblinka?* Said by *whom?* The things that could not be told to the lawyer, or at least not explained; that a terrible intimacy, which permitted Treblinka and bruises on the girl's skin, had been born in that stuffy, Bacon-like room, smelling of paint, tinkle of silvery rings on glasses, rasping pong of thinners, cluttered with unsold paintings and unread books and magazines, cushions stained and soiled, a Tunisian carpet representing the Garden of Heaven mushed into unrecognisability like a pattern in snow, newspapers, photographs, a framed poem by, he insisted, a young Parisian woman who was in love with him and who wanted to have his children, but that was twenty years ago and besides the wench was dead. Struck by a car and knocked off her bicycle – her wonderful long legs on that 'bike, the hot Paris breeze whipping up her skirt – on the boulevard Picpus, the respectable old ladies looking shocked because this beautiful girl's pink knickers showed as she lay in the street with blood pouring from her ears, the doors of a line of hotels opening and receptionists staring out as if a riot had begun, eyes frightened; the painter's eyes turned theatrically floor-wards, the recital continued after a respectful breath. *I should be burned at the stake! Do I look like the sort of bloke who'd crucify anyone?* Such mysteries and miracles and magicks to mourn over, a veritable grail of an exiled life. Until the cup of themselves had spilled over and nothing was permissible without a ticket of shame.

He lit a cigarette and read, turning it round and round, an advertisement for Campari printed on the tin ashtray. How many such as he had this room given witness to? It was a rather useless, not to say hopeless room, the paintwork smelling new and official, a table, the chair, repeating themselves endlessly in their ordinary forms, the very high window small and meshed with rusting metal, a sky too small framed a hundred times in its iron squares.

The door behind him was open and a guard paced outside, smoking, bored. There were other sounds, most of which he knew now as he might know the voice of old friends. Someone's reassuring shout, someone else's comforting swearing, a snip of laughter; you didn't have to understand a joke to know that it was a joke, it was in the voice of the teller. As sorrow was, when it came. The word *pâtisserie* came into his head unbidden; he smelled and saw cakes of exotic and lavish design, like precious objects imported from a distant island; he had been able to afford them, in any real sense, only when he'd earned his wages. The painter's goodhearted but naïve wink-and-nod good deed in a café bar named Le Lapin Vert, an insanely green rabbit or hare in wood over the front door, where he was expected to haul barrels and clean tables and wash glasses, reassured by the painter who knew everyone in the *quartier* that the owner was an old friend and a good sort; he'd lasted one week, knew the owner thought him a fool because his French was shaky and therefore almost ridiculous, the owner himself possessing not a word of English, a fat greasy androgynous figure, rubbery face entirely hairless,

98

in an open starry shirt that appeared to be too big and who smoked thin cigarillos all day; the two waiters laughed at him to his face, staring at him and cracking obvious jokes – well, no doubt here, one would say something, the other'd break up laughing – a local place where elderly men dated elderly women and attempted an intimacy both staged and indulged; no tips, everyone knew he was Irish and at the end of seven days they were calling him in English, *Shamrock*, which came out like shum-*rogg*. He'd wearied down into a basement, a dungeon, with a Quasimodo-like resignation, a thousand feet below the streets of Paris where everything dripped and squeaked and rats haunted the darknesses behind ancient empty casks, and here he attached plastic tubes to beer barrels and gas canisters and pretended for as long as he could, which mercifully wasn't long, that he was now living an Orwellian existence he could be proud of, among the people, not merely a remote intellectual of the Irish barroom kind. He despised them, anyway; he had been in the front line. An old soldier having little time for conscientious objectors. One day a waiter, following him down into the basement, most likely for a dare, had offered him the address of a kiddie porn website, even shown him some badly-printed pictures of children in frightened, drugged attitudes of sexual obedience. Perhaps that had done it for him, made up his mind, that he was considered to be that kind of person, up for anything, a stranger willing to be compliant to make friends, who knew? He went up the mediaeval ladder into the bar and told the owner he was leaving, *finis*, and up the ladder behind him came, not a bit sheepishly, prints still in his hand, the waiter, and the lard-faced owner had looked at him, appraised the situation, shrugged, reached into the till and handed him one hundred and fifty euros and told him, though he couldn't understand a word, that he could go now and fuck his baby brother, that's what someone got for doing someone a favour. Drained, he had returned early and found the painter working and explained, the painter, without once removing the brush from his canvas, nodding and grunting and finally saying that even the title of the café has a strangely pornographic ring to it, if you thought about it, he was sorry things hadn't worked out, such places were two a penny. He told the painter the whole episode had unnerved him. Rome, London, any big city, you'll find the same or similar, the painter had said. A dribble of white paint ruffed the scar on his nose. Not taking his eye off his work, not leaving his world. The owner is a cunt, he'd told the painter, trying to provoke a reaction. Literally, the painter responded; he's a woman, if you ever noticed a fat woman in there, that's Amélie, her partner. Imagine the movie *that* would make!

There was a rustling of feet, a crackling of doors. Small voices approached. He raised his head as the advocate – no, *avocat* – came in, marvelling at the man's efficient and down-to-business style which was always opened by a child's smile; not at all like the grimaces in those photos in the basement, not at all like those, thank God. The door was closed over upon them, a polite clicking of a lock. The man opened his briefcase and took out his cassette-recorder. The room was hot and the *avocat* shouted with alarming authority for water. A carafe and two glasses arrived. The water was warm and tasted of iron. There was a short, respectful, almost sacramental silence that reminded him of a confessional, just a second or two after the door clicked over; a set of papers emerged in front of him, one of which he saw as his signed confession, a copy of which the Irish representative, for what good he'd been, also possessed. In moderately accented English, and a deliberate school-masterly tap of his finger, the *avocat* drew all his attention sharply to the papers.

"The more I read this, Monsieur, the less I can ever believe it."

Ah! A silence developed between them, or was deliberately, tactically, allowed to develop; he shrugged his shoulders.

"C'est vrai."

"Let's try English," the *avocat* said.

"Yes."

The *avocat* shifted the papers, shuffled them, though there seemed no point to it; he glanced towards the door, then upwards towards the grilled sky.

"You pushed him down the stairs," said the *avocat.*

"Absolutely not. It happened as I've written there."

A wide refusal separated them. It seemed to go on and on. The tiny wheels of the recorder turned and turned, drawing in the empty air, the small distant sounds of a Paris prison. The water in their glasses, in the plastic carafe, grew warmer and less drinkable. The *avocat* looked tired and abstracted. Then he said:

"You saw what happened, what the girl did, you pushed him down the stairs. To make some sort of an accident. No?"

His mouth was dry. He looked across the grey mileage of the table and saw a mild, helpful man, troubled in himself, looking back at him, with his hands extended palms-outwards in a very Gallic way.

"You had watched, you had witnessed," said the *avocat.* "You thought what you thought. It was crazy! You handed the magistrates your guilt! How often have we wished to sacrifice ourselves!"

"No!"

"It's a form of suicide, it is not noble. The magistrates will not consider it noble. They will bury you alive. All the evidence.... an accident, it was almost laughable. You have to open yourself to me, M'sieur."

Again, a silence like water filling a jug. *Take me with you,* her eyes had said, or perhaps he'd missed something in translation. The dapper man across the table was trying to help, but he had no desire to be helped. A headache grew over his left eye.

"I have never been to your country," said the *avocat,* as if the time had come, the absolutely right moment, to discuss taking one's holidays. "After twenty years in such a place as this, Monsieur, you will have forgotten it ever existed."

Now, thought the *avocat:* how brave you are, how assertive! Let us speak in high voices of magistrates, of evidence, of certainty of conviction, process and prosecutions! You wear a different coat in here, where the weak and despairing are open to you, they can offer you no threat. He thought of Marcel, that damned bloody novel! Why did everyone have to lie in the face of overwhelming.... well, sometimes there wasn't always evidence as such, hunches, more than anything else. Equally, every bit, as devastating.

He wanted quickly to be out of the room, the prison, this flurry of stupidity and confronting Marcel in full view of that cursed restaurant, where, no doubt, he flirted with waiters and made a fool of both of them; what a life! Who had given him that novel? Some Beur? Someone in the street?

Why did the novel disturb him so much, did he really think Marcel would love him less – even need another man, one who could discuss such things as identity, being a French Arab, his head on his shoulder as revelation after revelation burst out of their mouths, their fucking pricks, for that matter – for reading a book that had a relation, however tenuous, to his own culture – *he* hadn't got a culture, he was as French and Parisian as the next man.

What would he learn inside the alchemical pages of an Arab novel that would make him somehow less French, transmute him into something that could not love only him, that needed the addition of more and more knowledge, such threatening knowledge, he wouldn't be merely an intelligent waiter anymore, and what was all this about the poetry, where was that leading?

There was the sound, musical, cool, of water being poured, Across the depressing table, the Irishman was pouring from the carafe and looking at him as if he'd never seen him before.

In small villages, thought the *avocat*, an ordinary man, today or tonight, will attempt to rape his daughter, or will murder his wife. Those one-street hamlets of sandy brick and statues, aeons old; of the Virgin in niches above appallingly ancient doorways; behind the shuttered windows, the heat always the enemy, nothing and everything passed time. They seemed always to be asleep – or charmed, or entranced – yet events touched them, every village with its plinth or obelisk; and over them all, just at the point where stone scraped the sky, a rusting iron French cockerel stood out proud and mute; dogs barking in invisible hazy distances behind those impenetrable crude mediaeval walls, the red slated roofs, the cold churches, ancient doors always locked, their stones speckled with pigeon feathers as if, finally, after too much torment, they had decided to grow feathers themselves, become great ornamental birds, and fly towards a paradise of which they had witnessed not a glimpse upon this unholy earth.

And as if to mock a docile heaven, some of them even had black bell towers that leaned and twisted, raped by weather, looking more dangerous than spiritual. Inside, pagan carvings leered from the chipped stone pillars; farm communities, working to a natural clock, often to a natural order the justice system could not fathom, yet had to deal with. The tranquillity of a volcano hung over some of those deserted places with their three-word names, and a child would disappear suddenly, like a break in good weather, or a man would shoot his elderly wife; he remembered anxious, mean crowds, local police knowing everyone involved and handling things badly, those days when he was always carrying a baguette in his bag and watching others, the more experienced, the more astute, practise a version of French law in places more suited to the rule of an Avignon pope.

Now the recollections had a particular power, and he couldn't rightly say why: he looked across the tomb-grey table and saw a village intellectual, a cunning man who'd read books and formed opinions which had set him apart. Even knowing his client had spent most of his life in big Irish cities – were they parochial too, yet in a bigger, larger way? – didn't alter the notion, appealing to him, that he was a country boy who'd had big ideas, had wanted to change the world – well, who hasn't? – and was probably a *flaubertois* by any other name, now drifting in the great city that was Europe, prone to deceptions, easily taken in and all that. Tenuous, but better than nothing.

"Would you like some?"

His client was, at least, mannerly. That counted. He recalled the hats-in-hand village mobs standing among their slightly battered Deux-Chevaux or capable Renault and you could always tell the prosperous ones by the way the others looked quietly hatefully at them.

"No, *merci.*"

"Such a strange word, that. Like the English, *Mercy.* As if greeting someone were the same as hoping he wouldn't chop your head off."

The Irishman pulled a cigarette from a packet of Royales, all defensiveness, showing off because that was the human thing to do in circumstances like this. The health warning's black lettering, ominous and final, caught the avocat's eye as the packet opened and bent:

Protégéz les enfants: ne leur faites pas respirer votre fumée

Other peoples' smoke was everywhere, it didn't just emanate from cigarettes, it came from their eyes, the words they spoke, the little deceits, and it was bad for one's health, eventually. Especially if one remained a child.

The *avocat* walked off in his head around the old churches, took stock of their unreadable headstones, thought of how new and better the world had been made, in the image of intellect and common sense. He believed, he realised, in absolutely nothing. He saw the ugly gargoyles clearing their throats of rancid rainwater and he sweated in offices no bigger than confessionals; testimony to this and that, who was where and so on. Then there were the big inviting windows with their farmhouses (renovated) and old mills (a little work needed) and even here and there a fag-end of a dead chateau; everything for sale or rent, the estate agents' windows were like Christmas trees to the retired or the young with money; leaning down on all of them, the leprous gargoyles with their knowledge and their secrets, like villains who hadn't yet seen the inside of the interrogation room. Villages so beautiful they were Monets, Manets, poems, romantic novels in their own right; yet, underneath all that ink and paint, the rough fibre of what made the human ugly. The local chess and *pétanque* clubs, the fairs, the gun associations, the rivers where the water never, ever moved. Behind everything – but, for the moment, a hero or devil, either way assuredly passing into village legend – dark as a blot on white silk, a surly client, cuffed and looking like a chastised schoolboy – the blood of a child, or another man, not dry on his thick hands; once a policeman, having nothing better to do, had pointed across the empty street to a gnarled tree and said it was a thousand years old, as if anything like that could possibly matter, yet here was a village copper contemplating Time. Somewhere-sur-Somewhere Else; Pont Anywhere-sous-le Grand-Anything; Chateau-Ass-Fuck-des-Anges: so many villages dumb with the burden of stories untellable.

And now when he looked across the table – wasn't it a wonder how quickly a man's mind could change? – he saw a smart-aleck, scared but holding his own or trying to. The cockiness of the prisoner who is, for the first time in many hours or even days – but not in this case, this called for special treatment, the Irish were watchful – holding a real conversation about something that interests him. The *avocat* was thankful for motorways, which cut past and over and round those little places of sudden sin. He could drive up to see his mother without, really, having to see them at all, save from safe distances. So a kind of cockiness fell on him too, and he leaned forward a little – just a little, an angling, an old trick – and breathed quietly into his client's pale and glistening face.

"M'sieur, let me be..... honest?"

The Irishman nodded. The *avocat* could smell his fear, its acid-and-nicotine reek. *You think keeping a secret will redeem you?*

"No," the *avocat* corrected himself, and he could see this threw his client, this linguistic precision, this desire to be formal and scrupulous. A nice little distance grew between them. Then he said:

"Let me be *frank*. You will not enjoy spending your life in a French gaol. You will soon lose your appetite for martyrdom. You will grow old and regret everything. Even her. If you are lucky, things will not go too badly once you have acquired a wife or become a wife yourself. I must tell you that, if you wish, you can make a report that I intimidated you speaking this way, or something like that. It doesn't concern me. Report me to your Irish representative, for the matter of that. But this is not a game, M'sieur. Briefly, your photograph will be in the newspapers; briefly, there will campaigns for your release at home, growing smaller and quieter until they merely squeak. But you would, on all the available evidence, appear to have murdered a French citizen, for the old painter *was* a French citizen."

The *avocat*'s hands were upturned and open, a parody of himself, perhaps, but he thought he had done a good job. The Irishman sat back in his chair and looked at him. And then he started to cry. Slowly, fighting against it of course – he would have to learn how to do that, a weeper gets the ass-fuck shower-rooms or becomes an object of barter; safely distanced from the horrors of prison's underlife, he and his colleagues had nevertheless made their whispered acquaintance with its social rules – but then came these little silver rivers, silver even in the graveyard light of the interview room. You had to understand that your client, whoever he might be, held on to a certain foolish bravado and that had to be worked on, chipped away, so that you could remould him for his contrite and humbled appearance in court. The more intellectual they thought they were, the more terrible the prospect of imprisonment seemed. He'd once known a real hard-case who, when he'd cajoled with a similar speech, had stood up, laughed loudly, pulled down his trousers before the guard could reach him and with his two hands opened his buttocks: *Maître, I've been married a few times before!*

The *avocat* felt, of course, the gathering aftertaste of self-loathing that always came with this sort of dramatic display of strategy. Someone like him to be in possession, suddenly, of so much emotional power, it was blasphemous, and when he thought for no apparent reason of Marcel – did such thoughts *obey* the laws of reason? – he appreciated that he too had the willingness to weep, but could his client, at his utter mercy, reasonably be expected to sympathise?

The Irishman's head was down now, all cockiness gone. The *avocat* thought: would I do as much for Marcel? Or would he do as much for me? The face of the *commissaire* in charge of the case came into his head, a poster-sized thing, floating in a jellied black emptiness.

"When the police find the girl, and they will find her soon enough, she will tell another story. A true one. Perhaps you will be thankful to her. I'd say you should kiss her feet."

The *avocat* stood up and nodded at the guard, and, all jelly-legs, strolled towards the door as casually as he could manage, then out of the room wanting to scream, plead for forgiveness, vanish into the stone cold of an ancient church and prostrate himself before an altar where none but the very old worshipped anymore. He tried to recall the *commissaire's* name and, ridiculously, he couldn't.

The iron speech of gated doors and their rough syntax shut behind him, the welcome knowledge of the rescuing distance he was putting between himself and his client and the consequent approach; however tediously; of cleaner; brighter air; did nothing to alleviate a sudden gust of nausea. A tender; almost exquisite dizziness fell over him, the weight of his slender briefcase was too much. He leaned against a Napoleonic door and the sight of an *avocat* in distress puzzled and paralysed strong and life-toughened warders upon whom the sight and sound of a prisoner losing his mind did not disturb a single hair. The *avocat* felt a surge of fatigue, then a gaseous but empty thing rolled about in his belly, like something grotesque waiting to be born.

At the same time, the blood seemed to plunge, cascade, from his head; he wondered whether he had turned completely white. Was he in the throws of a stroke? He muttered the single word, *God*, under his breath, closed his eyes and straightened himself. In the street, a beautiful blonde girl in tight, low-slung jeans was carrying a small black plastic bag of rubbish to a young man filling up a rubbish-van. They smiled at each other, made one another laugh. Warm city air washed over the stricken *avocat*. There was an odd tightness in his throat.

For a long, tremulous moment, he could not remember his own name.

A trembling, like leaves about to fall from trees in Autumn; a memory which was less than a wisp of thought, weightless, ghosting, of blue shutters whose paint peeled under the lash of an enormous sun and balconies from which old familiar women with their hair tied into buns looked on like deities at the street unfolding below them.

Then it was all gone, and she felt the sad hard jag of stone against her cheek and imagined she had slept with a vague but terrible monster, who, having fucked her, had himself turned to stone; as if she had that taint within her somehow, to do that to a man once he had spent himself, shuddered himself into her and was so tragically vulnerable, they always were at that moment, victims of their own lust, a satiated man turning back into the earth.

Cold, too. She opened her sticky eyelids to a rush of high trees, all that natural, frightening motion, threatening. The sky had turned darker and angrier, and she could smell rain in the air; soon it would hammer the leaves, cause some of them to fall off, perhaps bury her in them. She would never be found here; no one looks for the living in a graveyard.

She couldn't recall his face – this was not a sign of any malfunction, it was normal enough – and naturally did not know his name, the young man who had sold her whatever it was he had sold her, for she could not recall that either. It had knocked her out, obviously for some hours; she had had sense enough to pull herself into the shadows of an enormous tree and, of course, the decorous tombs, the astonished angels, the memorial heads, all protected her too. A delicious sense of self-satisfaction, she had saved herself, known what to do, where to go; even in a city of the dead there were ghosts stranger than anyone could imagine, who flitted from tree to tree, tomb to tomb, gate to gate, and who never tired, never slept, who always managed that soft and quiet act of redemption – the almost religious iconography of a hand outstretched, palm-upwards, *Take this and eat* – which was both sin and forgiveness in one act, which not even God could promise; without them, such child-faced, nervous demons, she would not live long but would crumble into the earth like dried-out leaves, withered by the ordinary air.

She wanted to sleep some more, but she knew how to use the remnants of a chemical fatigue to move on, her nerves quieted, her steps numbed. You could travel a considerable distance on this leftover lethargy, this little bit of sleep like something on the side of a plate, to be savoured for just a little while longer, and only as the hunger returned.

In the green distance, very far down the long, cobbled street – yes, it was a street, this was a city, and perhaps if she knocked at the gates of one of those elaborate tombs someone would answer, greet her, *Where have you been? You've been away so long!* – those people who had passed her by, were now disappearing into the dusk, dragging their bright daytime colours with them, fading, fading, then evaporating. She tried to stand up and fell back against the tree, snagged her shin against the bone-cold stone of a tomb. She stood up on her next try, a child learning to walk, amazed and frightened, and she tried to brush herself down; she slid her jeans and knickers around her ankles, the underwear was soiled, she removed a bloody tampon, threw it among the graves, scratched about in her pockets, found a replacement, inserted it, felt disgusted for a second with the smell of herself, so tartly, brutally frankly herself, of blood and fluids for the making of children, those tiny sacs, eggs, the tube of flesh and its serrated, ribbed edges to suck and pull, how did anything ever emerge from such a confused arrangement of discharges and flexings, the smell of a man's cum was particular to itself, and if it spurted from a man you loved you cherished it, sticking your head under the tented blankets long after he was gone to sniff again that delicious salted scrap of ocean, taste it on the tips of your fingers, remember his face, his look, and then this which was what he had produced because of you, because of what you made him feel or believe; she needed fresh knickers and now it was falling evening and the shops would be shutting, on her feet now, never mind the discomfort, the odour of herself rising with her, the world could smell her now, she made her way on to the cobbles of the great city of the dead and, looking up to knock the pain and stiffness out of the back of her neck, she could see in the close distance the twin chimneys of the crematorium, the memory that the painter had an old torn-out picture from a newspaper of those two chimneys, or maybe they were different chimneys.

There were distinct voices which told off the hours; a light scream, a distant gasp, the rasp of iron on iron and the belly-clang of a gate shutting, a guard's voice in the far-away outside, a warder's voice hollow as the galleries and halls of the prison itself. There was laughter, struggle, the sounds of protest, and all at once a great insatiable darkness would click into place – it had always been there, the light here was nothing, a mirage, it couldn't conceal the dark – and some sort of image of the world in which he sat came slowly into focus as his eyes adjusted, a tiny movement of a muscle, a nerve here, a twitch of a gristly lens there, and the cell turned dark blue, gifted with a frail and incongruous starlight, if you were lucky, moonlight, a crescent of silver. He would sit in this peculiar comfort and smell the toilet as if it were a fragrance new-sprayed into a sumptuous room.

The switching out of the cell light brought with it an odd calm. Perhaps it is the same when a terminally-ill patient accepts his coming death. So much less anguish, at least you'd like to think so. This afternoon's encounter with the *avocat*, a man charged, after all, with defending him, only doing his job, had not unduly disconcerted him. There had been some mad thoughts, and it was always possible to hang yourself one way or another, but he no longer felt either capable of doing that or particularly attracted to the idea. A light had been switched off in his heart.

The slide of the Judas. No, he was not hanging in some ridiculous position from the bars of his single window or some stray pipe or other with his prick erect and a pool of shit under his arse. He lay on his bunk and listened to someone singing, a brief song shouted into silence by a loud authoritative voice, and in the silence he was with the painter and the girl when the rioting that was not real rioting happened and he had been thrilled by it, that electricity in the air humming like the pleasure of a communal soul; dark then too, or falling dark, and they'd come up out of some café or other where, the painter had told them, the goddess-turned-actress Sarah Bernhardt had supped, the whole city was full of that sort of thing, celebrity as history, it was exhilarating and rather pitiful at the same time to an outsider like himself; a meal paid for by the painter, a new shirt, stiff and obvious, a design in a wide style, the wires on the painter's chest, rings glittering, scar muted, some scent or other, his French loud and commanding as if waiters would know him there, but they hadn't seemed to. *A cigar, for the love of Christ! I sold a painting today!*

What he'd meant was he'd been handed a rare and mean cheque today. It was natural that he should spend it on his family. *The painting was fuck-all, really. But I got away with it. People'd buy anything once you label it right.*

Art reduced to getting away with it. Perhaps revolution was like that too. Any kind of protest or objection, any human act, for the matter of that. Something sacred brought down to a level everyone could understand; what snobby bastard had said that if one was about to enter the era of the common man, he'd have no part of it?

Odd thoughts, not unpleasant, speculative after a couple of glasses of house red and a decent meal, a chicken thing with a white wine sauce, the painter still cherished a gentle resentment that he had not stayed on at a job he had obtained for him personally through his contacts, even if the owner of the place was one of God's mistakes, the ingratitude of the young. Life is struggle.

"I knew *indecently* rich people in the art world in London. One drove an Aston Martin. Blue, it was, too. Cost him fuck knows how much. He said if I could paint a series of pictures of him banging his niece, who was about fifteen at the time, if that, I could have it."

The girl looked at the painter, looked down at her plate; she'd eaten like some small animal starved for a week. The painter turned directly to her and she lifted her head; he repeated the story in French, and it was not difficult to interpret a word or phrase here and there, but he seemed to have fuelled the tale with a voluptuous nastiness for her sake. She stared at his lips, they were wet and wormy, he had bad teeth, smoker's teeth. He reached one flashy hand high into the air.

"L'addition, s'il vous plait!"

No one came. So he continued talking about London in the good old days of expensive cars and a rich bastard's incest and how it washes over you when you're young. It was easy to see how deliciously, even voyeuristically, he had circled everything that time had to offer, how being shocked was never a possibility, how the heavy hand of Bacon – when he spoke of him it was always as *Francis* – and a couple of handicapped poets had shaped the conscience of a world barely a thousand yards square, and now he offered the sordid tales as a kind of confession where no contrition and no absolution was required, just ears; but the girl hadn't even a decent pair of those, so he appeared to grow angry, speaking into her eyes, as if that was a distraction he could not afford.

"I could drive back then, but you can't drive in this city, it's a madhouse. I should have painted the fucker. Things only mean anything when you're young. Big cars, for instance. *A big car is simply an extension of your prick!*"

The painter then grabbed his balls and jigged them, a lewd and pathetic gesture, before sucking grandly on the Freudian cigar. Blue smoke fumigating the space of the table, causing the girl to cough. The band was still around the cigar, like a garter on a Black woman's thigh. This time a waiter appeared, bill a small white square on a silvery tray the shape and size of a polite ashtray. For a moment it seemed as if the painter, for the Hell of it, would remove the bill and tap the ash off the end of his glowing priapus onto the little tray, well, what was such maliciousness worth and everyone was, besides, nicely tight and philosophical; but he didn't, reaching instead into his frayed jacket for a wad of notes. He tipped the waiter. The scar was like a wisp of neon.

"You should have been alive back then, my children! For the price of a bend-over you could have your summer free in Monte Carlo. I knew a bloke did that more than once, on a fucking yacht in Monaco, never left the harbour, came back black as the Ace of Spades with a career as a painter and a sore hole. *Merci, garçon!*"

The waiter moved off, the cigar ash grew. At other tables elegant elderly women, faces browned and creased as if in the final stages of mummification, jiggled expensive bracelets in the faces of well-groomed silver-haired men in similar and

113

varying degrees of decomposition, who lit cigarettes for their companions and nodded agreeably now and then, politely intense; they spoke in low musical tones as if rehearsing alibis and seemed peculiarly at peace at their tables, as if they had come there not so much to eat as to wait for death, no matter how long it took, they'd be satiated, comfortable, when it came. The hysteria of a passing ambulance rattled the big gay windows and wailed off into the city's bad heart.

"Hope he dies on the job, like some Pope," the painter said.

Outside, the smell of the cigar wasn't so strong, carried off over the river in a warm, soothing breeze. Flash young men darted about precariously on motorbikes or sleek cars, windows down, *thumpa-thumpa* rhythms going. Elegant Blacks in suits carrying briefcases and laptops moved like bearers of royal secrets from one doorway to another; an odd light, a luminescence from the sky and the water of the river perhaps, hung over the pavements. It was dangerous to try to cross the street. It was alarmingly fast-paced on the pavements too. They were all tipsy, the girl had his hand and the hand the painter wasn't using to abuse his cigar. She looked very young all of a sudden, as young as a lecher's niece; the painter was saying things rather than speaking and it was acceptable to walk along paying no attention. It occurred to him then that there had been no offers of trips to Monte Carlo for the halfway Jew-boy here, no bend-over, behind-the-wheel suggestions, even that sort of invitation hadn't come his way. No Soho sodomies and a few quick introductions to ignorant rich people who'd buy a dead rat if it had paint on it; nothing like that, it had been cold in the pubs, the great and the ludicrous, the exalted and the maimed, each doing his own thing while the I-hear-he's-one-of-the-Chosen-People sat on his hump and chewed his anger along with theirs.

And you could see it in him, hear it anyway, the loss, the sharp *unbelonging* which had characterised those days hung on him like a prayer-shawl even now; those paintings of his

114

were depictions of landscapes against which just about anything could be played out, their false extravagancies, showiness, ordinary Paris office-workers in tights, a widow who could afford plastic surgery or breast-implants modelling as a Temple Virgin. So each of his arcane paintings was a vision of a dreadful Soho-of-the-mind, where everything was made up, mascaraed, forbidden, burned, *Baconised*, and, according to what the painter remembered, some shit poet had discovered a word to rhyme with *gamahooched*.

So bird-fragile, the girl's hand. They walked across the street, watching the striding green man, somewhere high in the clouds above and behind them the great *Samarataine* sign was shining in letters of unearthly fire. The food had been heavy and buttery and winy, and it sat in the gut like a delayed pregnancy, you wanted to eject it, get rid of the discomfort, shit it out quickly. He was remembering what the painter could do to the girl, a vomity mix of anger and regret in his throat, when he heard chanting as of angels, out of nowhere, apparently, it was enough to make the painter stop them all dead, father to them all, protective.

Down the quay came marching a troupe of about a hundred young people carrying banners and along the pavements and crawling the walls towards them the CRS dressed like black Terminators, chewing gum like tough guys from 'Forties movies, armoured head to toe, so much testosterone it had the curious effect of making you feel attracted to them; clatter of batons on translucent shields, a slow and inexorable advance, the young people coming and coming, he remembered how that was, that feeling, that ennobling thing, that certainty, if that's what it was that infected the blood and made you do mad things, dangerous things; he studied a poster and couldn't understand it. It didn't matter, really. They came on, singing, chanting, loud as an army, yet the girls so beautiful, the boys so handsome, he half expected to see movie cameras appear on cranes and someone shout 'Cut!' The painter did not move, even when other pedestrians retreated from whatever was happening or not happening, and the girl simply stared. On a lamp-post above his head was a poster advertising a cabaret of Marlene Dietrich songs; then a drunk shouted an obscenity and was dragged away by an ordinary policeman, not one of the Schwarzeneggers. He leaned against the wall of the river and the sound of the chanting and shouting made him forget he'd let go of the girl's hand, when he realised it, it was as if he'd let go of the world.

He looked around, couldn't see the painter or the girl. Lightheaded, he approached the singers and the chanters and the bearers of placards, as he had done so many times before, wanting to be with them and not having the least idea why, the sheer intoxication of it, beyond alcohol, dissolving into what was created by the crowd, its single mind, the sheer beating heart of it almost visible through the ribs which were its young people.

Even as he crab-stepped forward, unsure as always of purpose and motive, the black moving statues of the Compagnies Républicaines Sécurité bounding down on him out of the corner of his eye – how he envied their power and presence! – he became aware, as so often before, of an energy rising in him which was really a rage, an anger of immense power, rooted in nothing he could imagine or define; as if it originated beneath the soles of his feet, deep in the earth, and merely used him as a conductor of water, gristle and bone so that it could take form in the world. Was this what it had always been? Was he a tool, as some had suggested often enough in smoke-cured pubs, of forces greater than he could ever imagine, and was the red-hot heart of the earth itself the source? Was there nothing left of himself anymore? Had a woman, lying beside him, finally come to see him disappear slowly even as he made love to her, the passion not his but borrowed, on loan from a blasphemous place of constant energy without direction?

He was moving towards them, the singers, chanters, banner-wavers; perhaps he stretched out his arms, perhaps he shouted something. He knew he was smiling. And they stopped and backed away, the police behind him invisible behind their lowered Perspex shields stopping too. He was stranded – the silence was like a gluey wall around him – and the demonstrators were backing away, walking backwards, smiling and shouting and he was nowhere at all, and the CRS behind him, black and shiny like shelled insects, were walking backwards too; a mating ritual, a Zulu war-dance, something no one had told him about, was happening and he'd never seen anything like it, was lost for understanding of it, stood like a fool or a clownish target abandoned in the middle, as if both sides recoiled from him, recognised something in him of which they would have no part. Back, back went the police, the smiling, shouting demonstrators, and more alone did he feel with their every step, the sound of them distancing themselves from him, his isolation becoming a sense of chill, of cold, as if a flick of breeze had licked up off the river and caressed him, it was ugly, he wanted to run to one side or the other now, it didn't matter which side, embrace them, beg them to continue, continue, keep the ritual going, if that's what it was or had become, this was all too ridiculous and even drunk as he was he could see that, realise that, take it into himself that he had been something they were not; he had wanted a riot, it was almost sexual. It was like looking up the legs of a pretty women on a 'bus. The anticipation; what was *there?* But she'd noticed him, had pulled down her skirt, given him a reproachful look; it didn't matter now, he needed rescuing from his own embarrassment. He looked at the faces of the demonstrators, those pretty French girls' faces, always more beautiful than the faces of Irish girls, always more welcoming, and their handsome boyfriends and companions in revolt; and he saw the CRS relaxing as if a thousand miles away, some of them taking out new sticks of chewing-gum, the shields down, smiles here and there, the riot-sticks, the boots embraced in strapped leather, the helmets, the visors raised now, the dance had been enough. The anger was leaving him – whatever mad spirit had invaded him had fled and, worse, was probably in a shadow sneering at him. Nakedness, self-consciousness of the heart; he had been betrayed.

A new thing possessed him; he wanted to hit something, not from anger, that was gone, had been taken away from him, but from sadness, weariness, a sense of loss. The violence in him had turned to sorrow. Perhaps that was the function of the dance, the forward-and-back symbolism, the for-and-against motion of the opposing forces had worked on the acids and various other juices of his innumerable glands as the moon works upon the tides; on the ebb, he felt the going out of him, the retreat, the spilling of enormous waves of feeling.

Finger-pressure on his arm; he would have welcomed the police, but it was the painter, angry and spitting, dragging him off the road.

"Don't get involved! Anything could happen to you!"

He wanted fervently to say that no, that wasn't exactly true, that not *anything* could happen because the things he had wanted to happen had clearly not happened. It was ridiculous and patronising to suggest, just like that, showing that benevolence, concern, that action could be provoked just by wishing it. He could wish as long and hard as he wanted, but even now, seeing the demonstrators breaking into bundles of nowhere-to-go-now people, smoking, bantering, he'd seen this sort of conclusion before now and perhaps should have understood, but he didn't, he knew that what he thought or wished for was of no relevance in this world. Perhaps everything was and had been this sort of dance, those hours of marching and being afraid, marvellously afraid, those airport roads bleak in Atlantic rain, the sky dead, eroding the fields and the fences and the police looking wet and uncomfortable, the coats of the dogs wet and sticky-looking, everything and everybody uncomfortable; a ritual, God help us, an *understanding*.

"I don't understand," he said.

Like an old man, he was out of breath. The girl looked

at him and there was not a ripple, not a tick of muscle in her whole face, nothing to show how she felt or how she regarded him. The painter still held his arm – the feeling of the painter's fingers on his arm made him want to scream, he had no need of rescue, besides, there had been nothing to rescue him *from*. The painter gave him a cigarette, they leaned against the cold wall of the river. The air, a moment before charged with what appeared to be, or had taken the form of, intensity, was now blank and breathable again. He did not know what he had witnessed. He smoked and shook his head. The vehicles of the CRS were loading up, moving away.

"One a week," the painter shrugged.

He meant well, of course, but this was not what he wanted to hear. They were walking all of a sudden, he felt very hungry as if some muscle under the heart and near the belly had been loosened, and he was sobering up quickly. The woman of Samara who had given Christ a drink of water was commemorated behind them still in those great letters, as if each letter had become an angel, in flames; the Eiffel Tower was a pointer of white lights, but it pointed towards an empty and infinite absence.

They crossed the Pont Neuf and pale, cold light swept over them from a passing *mouche*. They walked – or were directed – by the painter, who seemed to have had enough of the night and strode on with a rickety but leg-stretching gait. He pulled them behind him on an invisible thread.

On the Ile de la Cité the crowds of tourists, so many Japanese, English with Manchester United shirts on, as if suddenly the city had become something else, a tourist arcade, a place where Paris ended, where France dissolved; here, somewhere, they found a café that was still open, or open enough, some chairs glinting in a soft metallic light piled one on the other, and beside them a shop of appalling yellow glare showed off its shelves and hangers of miniature Eiffel Towers, small armies of gargoyles and dragons and demons which supposedly reflected the great stone holy nightmare of Notre Dame, handkerchiefs with 'Paris' scrawled on them, the cathedral in plastic domes, shake them and it snowed, and so many postcards, so many depictions, views, angles, jokes, efforts at being naughty; caves of key-rings, pens, fake perfumes, guidebooks, bracelets, slides, videos; it was all very depressing.

"If there was a *tabac* open, I'd do the Lotto, " said the painter. "I won twenty euro one time."

A waiter arrived. There was a hurried conversation between the waiter and the painter. The waiter shook his head. The painter's breath stank of drink and tobacco. Big Americans passed by wearing UCLA sweaters and baggy shorts. The painter stood up. The waiter disappeared.

"Won't serve us. Too late. *Cunt.*"

They continued walking. Fatigue set in, heavy eyelids, a staring at the pavement flags passing under them, an aerial view of dirty rice-paddies. His feet hurt. The air was melancholy and full of bits of lost conversation; everything was passing by, earnest, intent. The carved face of the great cathedral – observe Saint Denis, holding his head under his arm; beheaded, he'd picked it up and walked away, bored and saintly; observe the tiny walled cities in the arms of the saints, the precisely carved gates and towers, and the Heavens and angels of stone – was scrubbed white with light and in the dark crevices where the light became shadow tiny birds shifted uneasily. Kids were heading there, to the square in front of the cathedral, clutching skateboards. A Black girl with a twelve-string guitar and a cowboy hat on her head sang Donovan's 'Colours' in a wailing Carribbean voice under the iron-dark moustaches of the soldiers of Charlemagne, hauling the scowling great leader into the Parisian night on his black-iron horse. Somewhere off across the square, the *bumpa-bump* of a ghetto-blaster.

The mute, deaf girl took his hand. If the painter noticed, he said nothing.

In the drowsy warmth of a bakery, the *avocat* listened to the quick exchanges of the women around him and began what appeared to be an intimate inspection of the marvellous confections, the creamy wonders, the cherry-topped celebrations of the art, the angelic bakerings, all lined up on crisp beds of serrated paper with patterns as delicate as lace, all preening themselves under the thin glass of the bakery's cases.

His mind was very far away, in the prison, in his childhood, sitting at the side of his mother's bed, and he had no idea what he looked at, a respectable-looking man in a baker's shop full of busy women and the smell of expensive perfume.

Ten minutes walk away were the *bouquinistes* on the river, and he had a mind to give himself time to go there and browse among the dead magazines and the brown, ancient postcards of big-arsed women posing for a man in a top hat, in a corner of the photo a ubiquitous palm in a pot. He wanted to stroll about the stalls, take his time, immerse himself in the cover of a magazine from the 'Forties, or a clump of mouldering books on Napoléon. He wanted to buy a poster for his − *their* − bedroom, something arty and topical; a page from an illuminated music manuscript, the notes blocky and absolute, like a child's interpretation of God. When he imagined buying the poster he thought of Marcel and that brought a slow pain which opened in his belly like a sick flower. He wanted to see the river wind lift the pages of the old magazines and warp the faces of dead film stars and sports heroes.

Perversely − he knew his own sense of perversity well enough − he bought, when his turn came, two big cakes, runny with creamy custard in them, bright and shiny as paint, each the size of his outstretched hand. He could not purchase only one. It was, with Marcel, against his nature. That's what partners *did*, after all, they bought in pairs, in twos. His *portable* twitched in his pocket. The two confections were wrapped in a loving little box and he still hadn't paid for them. A pretty girl, her hair covered in a hygienic paper hat, waited for him with large and oriental brown eyes.

The women excused themselves with decorum and floated by him, through the open door, one by one, quiet now.

"Yes?"

Marie, in her formal voice.

"*Maître*, Madame Elias rang twice, and now she's in the waiting-room."

An odd weightlessness from the neck up, as if his head were filled with air or gas, and was about to ascend from his shoulders; he could barely ask the obvious question, could scarcely open his mouth. At the same time, he tried to appear calm and dignified in the middle of the shop; a public place, eyes on him.

"I had an appointment to meet her, right?"

"Yes. At five. She claims she has more malicious e-mails for you to read. She says you advised her it was almost time to contact the police."

Did I say that? the *avocat* thought, as his head drifted among the trees and over the river and on towards the peaceful, strolling plots of the Tuileries. *Did I advise someone? I have no recollection of anything. I do not know Madame Elias. Jewish.*

"What shall I tell her? She's angry. I don't....."

"Tell her my mother died this morning. I had to leave in a hurry."

"Your mother is dead, Hervé?"

"No, she's not. But it's a good excuse."

He giggled. *I am going mad,* he told himself.

The girl behind the display case had not moved. Now there was a sharp pain over his eyes as if some small animal were trying to push its way out and a light but discernible nausea crept upwards into his throat.

"Hervé...."

"Tell her that, Marie."

"I don't know if I can. Honestly, I don't know how *you* can. Poor woman!"

He hung up. He had neither the will nor the energy to debate the matter. He shut off his *portable* and turned to the girl. He paid her, lifted the little dainty packet, and vomited loudly and painfully all down the side of the glass.

"Ah, merde!" shouted the girl.

The contents of his stomach, in colourful swathes and bitty shapes like a strange Modernist painting, all over the floor, dripping slowly, as if he were melting, down the glass; it was all over his shoes, too. In one hand, miraculously, he held the cakes, in the other, the 'phone.

"Jesus!"

Now people had appeared from the back of the shop, from its hot innards, hot looking and rubbing their hands, wrapped in white with daubs of flour here and there. How many women, how many men, he could not make out. He found it difficult to lift his head. His legs were weak. Still, he held out the cakes, balancing them admirably. And his 'phone.

"Are you drunk, M'sieu'? Why didn't you just *shit* all over the floor, since you're here!"

Women's faces peering back in from the street: had they left too soon? Fat and round, with little interrogative eyes, not the elegant faces he'd noticed only seconds ago. Towels had materialised out of thin air, a bucket, water. Someone closed the front door. When the sounds of the street went away, the noise in the shop was very loud; cloth in water, the slither of more cloth across a floor. He smelled sweet disinfectant. He saw every cake and shape of bread in the cabinet in front of him dumped into a tray in wounded, mangled heaps. There was a great deal of coming and going all around him and it was as if he had become invisible.

"Wipe yourself, M'sieu'. Clean yourself up in the back, there."

"Madame Elias is waiting for me," he heard himself say.

"Her cakes will have to wait. Clean yourself up, now."

A big male voice, now, aggressive, heavy:

"La-*laah*! We are closed because of you, M'shieu'! Personally, I'll accept a cheque. *Give me those fucking cakes!*"

The cakes were taken from him. Someone was wiping his face with cold water. His head was coming back, returning with news of very distant places.

"I am very sorry. I just felt ill. I couldn't help it."

"Wipe yourself, forget about it. It happens."

A voice as soothing as his mother's.

She saw how the road and street signs, one stacked on top of the other, were from behind like the mislaid white keys of a piano. And how some streets, being wider than others, were like great sheets of water across which pedestrians tried to swim, hesitated, swam on a little more; each far pavement was a shore.

How they were looking for her, no doubt about it, how she could slip down among the guts and lungs and kidneys and livers and arteries of the city and be shat out somewhere else, reconstituted. And how an old man sat on a stone bench in a small park, the paving was sand and yellow stones and fed flock after flock of pigeons from his open hands and he brought his lips together, coo-coo, at the birds while they, fat with strange messages, wrote with their feet in a secret language.

There were child-angels stranded in the stone of small churches and one stone man, naked, strapped to a broken wheel as two impassive stone men turned it, turned it, and the breaking man cried out, she could hear him. Slim saints in stone, bearded stone faces that never, never laughed, their books open at some page the pigeons alone could read; walking on, she felt the weight of the evening sunlight, how pretty it made the buildings and the open shutters and the black wrought-iron balconies and the men in vests leaning out on them and the glimpse of a woman or a child behind them, how pretty, how potent as a memory smelled in the nostrils can be potent and just out of reach, the image. Laughing to read the hand-printed sign on a church door:

Seule La Prière Permet
De Communiquer
Avec Dieu

Ici le portable
Est Inutile

It made her laugh – of course the mobile phone was no way to talk to God! – someone had a sense of humour, but she laughed and laughed until a leathery door opened and an old woman emerged from the candly dark and admonished her, flick-flicks of the gnarly single finger. She walked away, a breeze from the river lovely here, the tourist shops, so many of them like birthday cards on a string on fire, bright as seraphic glory one ranked upon the other, their hierarchies of light, the river smelling like sugary melting ice-cream, the gulls nervous and irritated on the worn patches, the dog-shit piles, under the leafy trapped trees. She remembered them, saw them again, the painter waving his finger like the old woman. She had been proud of his dash into the crowd. The painter had grown suddenly very old, and parts, layers of his canvassy facial skin had begun to peel off in front of her lazy eyes like layers of paint, revealing the hard grey bone of his skull. They'd walked home, back to the painter's courtyard which was by then bathed in an artificial light which seemed to fall from the sky, into his downstairs room, the shock of such disorder, such ruin, half-drawn and semi-painted landscapes and figures and heads watching her, watching her, her hand let fall now, a bottle produced, a kettle, the painter's voice looking like a rusty saw drawn across the front of her brain and the young man standing to one side grinning as if he were watching them from somewhere above the earth, he had detached himself so utterly from her. She felt curiously angry at him, too.

Now in front of her there was a Chinese man seated perilously on a tiny foldable chair and his sign said: *Votre prénom en chinois – 10f.* But no one used francs anymore. The Chinese man sat in sandals, his feet close together, drawing out the symbols in which the pigeons spoke – they wrote with their feet, his calligraphy was the marks their feet made in the dust – and behind him two Black boys played guitars. Staring, then, at the dull and scarred iron street pole stiff beside him, in whose glaze she saw herself, her body stretched out; she was hungry now and the smell of cooking was all over the place. Along the river white blossoms fell from the branches of the trees. The evening was warm. They had sat down among the shipwreckage of paintings and drunk tea laced with cheap vodka and she had slipped two tiny Valium 5 tablets into her cup and the painter had noticed and said 'Stop that shit, for Christ's sake!' as if he had come to the end of something with her, needed a sudden morality, she'd watched the words clatter out like bits of barbed wire flung through the air, not like his tone at all, and he stared more and more at the young man and when they spoke their moving lips were like the feet of pigeons in the sand and pebbles. In that moment, feeling ignored, she had longed to walk alone by a river.

But she was thinking of balconies and children and a view of a river far away on another planet. She removed herself from the room, so that when the painter flung one of his canvases aside and stood up as if to hit the young man, then slumped down again, a heap of a human being, a rough stone come to life, a shadow with a shape poured into it, she was many miles away and could no longer see them.

Magazines in cellophane flapped like flags in the river breeze. Every stall was alive with movement; pages of books flicked and rose and fell, postcards burning in their colours in the hot air danced off their piles, stall-holders pursued them across the trenches of other books, other cards. Faces of dead film-stars twisted and turned in the air; the headlines of ancient newspapers – *La Guerre est finie! De Gaulle et l'Algérie libre! Belmondo à Londres!* – declaimed frantically about things that had no meaning for her. Here, a sheet of music, the notes in curious square-shapes; there, a picture of a small fat Napoléon beside a field-cannon. Black piles of old records, big as steering-wheels, tipped precariously against endless battalions of old books.

He materialised out of the ground. She turned to look up at him, always her eyes groping for lips.

"Fuck off. Leave the books alone. Get!"

She wondered if he could smell her, as she could begin to smell herself again. She wanted to go somewhere and tidy up, put in a fresh tampon. His shirt was covered in flowers. Their gaudy heads moved in the breeze. He glared down at her, a wide-shouldered man who hadn't shaved.

"What the fuck are you staring at? Buy something, *pépée*, or bugger off."

She continued to look up at him – did he not regard her as he would any other girl? Did he not wish to sleep with her? Why was he so quick to dislike her? What must he have read into her prolonged stare?

"You're titless – what age are you?"

Behind him, a picture of Elizabeth Taylor strained against the threads of string holding it to the canopy of the stall. The man looked away from her, seemed to look over every roof in Paris, far away, into the heavens. The flowers on his shirt nodded. She lifted up her shirt and showed him her breasts. She felt the slap of river wind on her skin. He looked. She was laughing at him now – at the nodding little flowers on his shirt – even as the side of his hand came down on her head; she stepped back, cat-quick, and the tip of his fingers nicked one of her nipples.

She pulled down her shirt. A couple of Japanese tourists stopped and looked. The man took stock of himself. She could see his lips, watched them wriggle like little worms, purple as the big vein on a hard cock.

"I wouldn't risk a dose!"

But the Japanese tourists did not speak French. They raised their cameras.

She walked off. Another stall-owner had come up now; the two men, she knew without turning round, would talk about her, shout things after her. She was beginning to plummet, going down fast. Tears would come soon. From nowhere, everywhere. She passed a little bakery, odours of baking bread, the half-memory of comfort far away, its window-trays strangely empty, where a woman splashed sudsy water through the open door. The woman pushed and pushed at the mop, the head of the mop a stringy wet wig. The woman looked up, the stench of disinfectant was strong. She was not old but her movements aged her. There was a picture in the painter's bedroom, torn from a magazine, of women bending to their work just like this woman, only they had been in a field. The woman dipped the Rastaffarian mop in her bucket again. In and out, a rhythm to her, her bright black hair tied neatly back. She raised her head again, looked at the girl.

"What's your problem? We're closed."

She wanted the woman to say something nice to her. It was a ridiculous, weak thought. She straightened herself up, reached into her bag, took out her box of tampons, indicated her mouth and ears and shook her head. The woman looked at her.

"Mother of Christ! It's up the stairs. Anyone asks, I didn't see you."

The bakery looked so empty, the shelves and display-cases should have been filled, piled high with cream-bloated miracles and honey-clotted incredibilities; in a corner, a stack of brown loaves, some croissants and a heap of cellophaned sandwich-rolls, like corpses on a battlefield. Once in the tiny closet she pulled down her pants, saw that her knickers had held up well, there was only the tiniest leak, removed the bloody tampon, washed herself with the green soap that squirted from a bulbous container above the sink, rolled the used tampon in toilet paper and disposed of it in the hygienic bin beside the toilet-seat. She was very tired now and took a strange pride in doing things that were clean and correct. She inserted a new tampon, soaped the sides of her thighs, washed them, dried them with more toilet paper. She washed her face, drew back her hair. She didn't look too bad. The nausea might or might not come. The dizziness was certainly on its way. She tossed back a tablet – not many left, have to do something about that – and washed it down with tap water. Feeling better, she left the closet. In the empty, raped-looking shop, the woman had finished up. She smiled and nodded at the woman in thanks.

"Here."

The woman handed her a fat cheesy sandwich roll wrapped tightly in cellophane. Then a brown bag of brittle croissants, three of them. Their wonderful oiliness made map-patches on the paper. She nodded again. The woman's face was pretty, or had been. She wore a lot of very light makeup but a mole stood out, resisting. The woman too looked tired, as if the mopping was a punishment for some regretted wrongdoing, a penance that had to be worked out, and would then be followed by another, the corner of a packet of Gitanes stuck out of a pocket and she had this tiny black mole beneath her left eye, so brilliantly black it looked artificial. It was very hot in the shop and she could see men in white overalls moving about behind swing doors. The woman tapped her on the shoulder.

"Take care of yourself."

Then the woman touched the top of her head with the flat of her hand, a blessing, an admonition, who cared? The woman's hand felt good in that light second or two. The woman turned her back and walked away, carrying her bucket and mop, into the back of the shop. Out on the street again, she felt her scalp begin to tingle, as if the skin wished to contain for as long as possible the angel-weight of the woman's hand.

A police car drove by slowly and she lowered her head. *Soon, soon enough.* There were thoughts coming through to her now, like signals from a distant place, and they were dark and heavy and unwelcome and made her sick. She rested herself in a doorway; how pretty the legs of the girls and women walking by! She looked up and saw clouds the size of mountains towering over the lake of the sky. She slumped down to a sitting position and unwrapped her sandwich roll. Across the street, a black rat ran out of a flood-drain and scuttled like a thief along the side of the pavement.

Elle se rappele. How the painter, then, standing, had been waving his hands around the room, indicating God only knew what, his paintings, she had supposed, but by then she was losing her grip – the young man standing there, a strange smile on his face, and not looking at her at all. How she could look at these paintings, at what he had made of her in paint, and almost hear the colours, that was a mystery and a miracle and a secret! Then – did time pass, or was time of any significance in that room? – sitting beside him on the devastated couch, the room spinning slowly as she dragged on a joint, the young man cross-leggéd on top of old newspapers, the snug feeling of it all, knowing this was where she was for certain that night, always a good feeling; and the painter's fingers slipping down the back of her knickers, one finger probing the gentle slope into the crack of her arse, she had started to giggle. She stood up, did some mad wriggly dance in front of both of them and took off her clothes, it was so hard to manage that, while they watched her, she saw the young man's eyes eat her flesh. She danced in front of him, moved the thick black wad of her bush in front of his face, letting him breathe her in, the painter was down behind her now, kissing the cheeks, his breath hot there, the young man in front of her lifting one hand and spreading its five fingers across her belly as she moved and moved, feeling the hunger of the men, their need, their mindless adoration, why were they always so easy? The young man's fingers had found the lips of her slit, dry as old paper, she was far away from them, felt nothing, danced as if she were stumbling in a dark room, saw them pulsate, felt their

130

breath on her skin, her own power over them terrible and ugly and irresistible, the only power no one could ever take from her acknowledged in every touch of their mouths and fingers on her, the young man standing up, looking at her in a strange way as if to say something but nothing came out but his ridiculous brown cock from his trousers and, awkwardly, in a laughable position, he pushed it between her thighs. It could find nowhere to go, had no power to go anywhere, the painter grabbed it where it emerged, everyone was laughing, the young man tried again, more seriously, more violently this time, banging bone against bone, hurting a bit but that was to be expected, she tilted her hips to help him and the painter fell down behind her on his face, she turned and he was laughing wildly, a bottle of something had fallen over and its contents stained a large swathe of newspaper, the young man was helping himself, his hand moving over his stupefied prick and his face as guilty as a child's caught stealing an apple, oh, how funny-sad men could be! The young man came, sweating, white-faced, almost fainting with the effort, in a creasing of his forehead and the runny egg-yolk on her belly and slipping over his fingers and he trying to flick it off, falling back, his eyes closed, into the moment of his swarming shame, all of them the same, the steam gone out of them, they were afraid of themselves and couldn't imagine their own sinfulness, the painter throwing up, a sound the shape of a wall, *Haaaarughaawwwlpt!!!* and she stopped gyrating then, dressed herself as if they'd paid her and perhaps they should have and she slumped down on the couch, the stickiness of the young man pressed into her flesh by the tight cloth of her jeans. She slept. When she woke up, cold, depressed, shivering, she crossed the dead courtyard under a cynical blue dawn light that skulked in every corner, out of every shadow, going up to the painter's bedroom, an airplane a winking red star a million miles above her head going off across limitless seas, and it was there that he, waking up as if alerted to some great danger or threat, struck out at her first with his hand, then with his fist and when she ran away from him, unable to make out one word his wet lips made, knowing this would happen, she was hardly innocent, God knows, the painter always went away from himself and came back to himself with fury, and he kicked her, both of them naked, the smell of her sweat and the ammoniac residue of the young man and the painter stopped suddenly in front of her, the blue light beyond the single window brightening, brightening, the colour of duck's eggs, his hand suddenly thrust between her legs grabbing, pulling, squeezing, she had looked into his lips and he had shaped a few words, *Putain! P000taannn!* his French barely discernible on the dribbly slugs of his lips, the white stains at their edges. And when he'd let go of her his silver-ringed fingers had been covered with her blood.

She tried to eat the sandwich-roll, it was difficult, her throat was raw and sore as if she spent her day shouting. The downer helped but the food, she knew, would not, a bag of *la chnouffe* was too expensive, at least for now, but she'd get some; the processes of digestion would have a sobering effect, however gentle, and she could not afford that. She threw the good, well-meant sandwich across the road and a police car slapped past her – she remembered that she really was too close to the Préfecture de Police, it was not wise to wander without some sort of purpose or direction, but she had none – she almost hit the vehicle with the roll, its lights clicking in the warm air, something urgent, but she thought it better to move. She got up, her legs hotly painful where she'd squatted down. From nowhere a sharp pain crossed her belly, then another, and she had just enough time to pull down her trousers, there in the evening sunlight while the pretty women walked by, ignoring her, and another rat scumbled off out of a sewer, she in a respectable doorway within a dash of the misshapen towers of Notre Dame shat a lumpy brown liquid which smelled acidic and terrible, and she wiped herself crudely with the oily croissant bag, the contents hastily tossed out, waddling off then down the street as if nothing had happened, ashamed of herself, crying openly, not caring who looked at her, while a 'mouche glided down the river past the stately solidity of the Palais de Justice and the cliffs of the lawfully indignant quai des Orfèvres like a swan; the tourists on the decks shouted and waved at the city and the splayed iron of the Eiffel Tower looked, in the distance, like a thin woman opening her legs behind some hedges to pee gigantically, enough to flood the Seine.

Marcel in the kitchen humming to himself, making a warm salad, the heat in the place was stifling anyway, the windows were open and it made no difference, the traffic outside was loud and it seemed to raise the temperature, the *avocat* helped himself to a cold beer and absentmindedly watched his lover, the arcs and bridges of his body, the sweat moving over his naked torso and the rigidity of the muscles in his upper legs. Marcel wore only boxer shorts. The *avocat* had found him like that, working at the stove. There were several kinds of cheese on a chopping board, mushrooms and other things, such as balsamic vinegar. Marcel now and then stopped what he was doing and pulled on a slim joint. The room was dangerous with the combined breaths of marijuana and cooking oil sizzling in a pan. The *avocat*, convinced that he had a terminal illness, even one picked up from Marcel, felt the dull increased thudding of his nervous heart and tried to concentrate on the pages of *Match*, which normally he would never buy.

The magazine was too glossy, too fast for his tastes and the celebrities meant nothing to him. He'd found it skulking under a chair and supposed Marcel had purchased it, but this, like so many other small things, could not be verified. As well as dying, he was moving into vague and betraying areas of doubt about this, that and Marcel, and such a state of uncertainty and unknowing naturally contributed to his nervousness. Tonight's concert could be ignored, of course, but he was reluctant to put it off in case Marcel suspected something, or suspected that *he* suspected something. *I am dying,* he wanted to stand up and announce; *and fuck you and your secret lover, I just want you to know that I know!! I want you to make* him *sick too!* The wretchedness of his thoughts depressed him further. He had proof neither of his lover's betrayal nor of his own impending doom. He felt angry, visions of being sick on the bakery came back and back and back, he could not clear his head of them, the ignominy.

"Is this *tenue de soirée*? You know how these things terrify me and I always imagine I'm improperly dressed. I wish I *could* go improperly dressed."

"No," the *avocat* said wearily. The phrase carried something ponderous in it, suggestions of extravagance and sweating chandeliers. Marcel enjoyed such phrases. "It's merely a concert of music, for anyone."

"In such *religious* surroundings! My God! I was only once at a concert in a church. Pure theatre! The Mass as a three-act play. I think I was twelve at the time. Oscar Wilde said the Mass was theatre. By the way, someone has suggested, *in my hearing,* that they know where the penis off Oscar's sphinx is. The things you hear in a restaurant. I can tell you, *mon maître.* I wanted to laugh. Perhaps I'll dress like *this.*"

The *avocat* said nothing. Marcel camped up, and made himself absurd, quite deliberately. A challenge of sorts. *Would you be seen dead with a whore-queen like me? Con!*

"What's wrong with you?"

"Nothing at all."

"You're too quiet. That's a bad sign. The moon's up."

"I have a particularly difficult case at the moment."

"The whole city knows about that. That's what you *do,* after all, and it makes you *glow.* Have you thought that perhaps he's a terrorist, an Irish terrorist, what are they called?"

"No, he's not."

"Well, maybe that's a pity. Imagine the publicity of that if he were. Better than fucking. *I* could do with that sort of pub.... Is that all that's bothering you?"

The *avocat* answered by going to one of the long windows and looking out into the street. He heard screaming again, the shock of horrified spectators. If he died, killed in a monstrous pileup, a painful blockage somewhere down in the intestines of the *périphérique*, how long before Marcel exhibited his lover on a street just like this one, poncing his arse in tight designer slacks, exaggerating the swing provocatively, everything a damned display, a show: as if, in Paris, anyone would notice? Or cooked for a new man, half-naked, while smoking a joint? So comfortable in the relationship that there was often nothing to say? Or so cocky that the feeling of power stopped his mouth?

"Do we have time to eat? Grant me that at least."

"Yes," the *avocat* replied.

He was thinking of his mother, his mother lying in a bed attached to a variety of machines, the machines keeping her alive. Did she know enough to be afraid? Did the nurses bring flowers – robbed from someone else's bedside, drooping a little, ashamed from being passed around too much – so that the smell of death would not utterly wash the walls of the room? Was there a view from the window? Was there still a window?

Marcel washed and chopped, the gleaming knives efficient and alive in his dark hands. The *avocat* hated washing-up; it was not the chore itself but the irritating and disappointing minutiae of the work, not the washing of a plate but discovering, wet cloth in hand, that there was no washing-up liquid, or not enough of it left in the squeezable bottle, or that the water had turned cold suddenly and greasy things stuck immovably to cutlery and crockery. He avoided it whenever possible. Marcel's hands, then, swift and agile, like small fussy animals independent of the rest of him, twitching here, angling there, grasping something, opening, letting something go, hypnotic movements, lovely, ritualistic, holy over the sink, the cutting-board; in the street someone was talking loudly, the sound of the words moving past the open windows like a painter's brush across a canvas. For want of something better to do, he leafed through the pages of a local free paper, something that was always and regularly pushed into the row of letterboxes in the hallway. Here a book-fair, here a jumble-sale, there a long list of lonely men and women looking for love or sex or both, there a ranked gallery of plain Black faces, overdressed smiling men in shirts and ties, advertising the ineffable, the mystical, the healing of the soul, or an end to the bad luck which had made a life almost unbearable. *Dr Hakim — Palms Read — The Future Revealed — Consultations by Appointment Only.* Some of them were brazenly elaborate: *Sister Aisha — See the Past and Future! — Cures for Arthritis, Phobias, Smoking — Spells for Good Health and Success in Love Cast — Sacred Potion! Dr. Abdelmalik Kousa — A Final Cure for Tiredness and Fatigue! — A Cure for Impotence and Drug dependency! — Hypnotism for Fears of Heights, Flying, And Etc! — Consultations.*

What was death but a final cure for tiredness and fatigue?

An entire page and a half of these faces, offers, declarations: he laid the paper down on the couch, small mousy rustle as it settled there, Marcel in someone else's arms, the thought of it, perhaps a visit to Sister Aisha, or Sidi Moussa, a cure, something to place under Marcel's pillow; there was a world running hectically beneath the world he lived in where things were very simple, really, where love was a small bag of powder and the future was a handful of chicken bones: a not unattractive place, surely.

He went into the bedroom and found his tape-recorder, reels like ratty eyes, set it on the bed, turned it to *Play* and while it spoke to him, like a voice from a grave or out of the air, he undressed, began choosing shirts. Marcel was singing *Love Me, Luuuuve Me* and the *avocat's* voice cracked up, tinny and drunk with static, his pleading injunctions across a bolted table in a bolted prison room: *How often have we wished to sacrifice ourselves.* Choosing a shirt, laying it on their enormous bed, it fell like a man collapsing, he thought of himself throwing up in the bakery, a fluttering of fear, trapped little bird, in his breast, maybe he should tell Marcel and watch his face contort with guilt, you've made me sick, condemned me, you unfaithful crossbred Beur *fuck*, you've probably buggered have the Marais and back, styling yourself one of the bad boys, you're just a well-tanned whore, pissed or stoned or whatever, I should lift one of those knives and cut off your prick, I'd get away with it, crime of passion, two-a-penny waiter writing shit poems and probably fucking the editor of that magazine, what's-its-name....

Marcel entered the room and handed him a glass of deep red wine, wine rich as blood, a hint of splintered cork pimpling the edges.

The *avocat* stood there in his bare chest, a simple silver crucifix Marcel had given him rested against the silvery-haired flesh, his voice came out of the tape-recorder and he should have been listening to it, wondering about the *dossier* – imagining how his learned opponent, *juge du parquet* Saloman, merciless by reputation, ridiculed privately as an *Israelite* and for his name but he was both wise and dangerous – family reputed to be the among the oldest citizens of the Marais, had two brothers, black-draped, bearded, hair in side-bangles, who wouldn't speak to him, Hasidim – would skewer him, he'd known strong men to leave the court sweating and pale under a grilling from Le Grand Juif, as he was quietly known – instead of the voices in his head.

Marcel kissed him lightly on the forehead. The *avocat* stood there, vulnerable, feeling angry and stupid. Marcel walked with that gleaming look-at-me stride back to his sink, his singing, and the *avocat* wanted to fuck him then more than anything else in the world. But Marcel seemed untouchable, a man within a man; he went back to his clinical fiddling with balsams and sprigs and spices, an alchemist, Oriental and therefore mysterious. The distance between them grew intolerably, until the *avocat* lusted to throw his glass of wine at the tall young dusky man assiduously peeling and sorting at his sink, reassure himself that, if he were indeed untouchable, he was not unreachable. He imagined the wine flowing down Marcel's body like blood from a terrible wound. He saw how easy it was to murder. *Love me,* sang Marcel. In English.

When Marcel called him to the table – it seemed as if an age had passed, that Paris had been torn down and rebuilt, the *avocat* locked off his recorder, unable to remember one single word, feeling defeated and unworthy, Saloman would eat him, all that sort of thing, a small sad lump in his throat – Marcel served up a good salad and settled a new magazine in front of him. The *avocat* looked up.

"Something light," Marcel said. "There's lardons, we have cheese, there's bread cut up in the basket, the omelette's on the way. Don't complain."

The *avocat* felt like a big child being scolded. He had not intended to complain. Rather, he would have wished to eat alone. The lump in his throat was tight now. Perhaps he had cancer. Perhaps he would not be able to swallow.

He dished salad on to his plate, a tang of vinegar licked his nostrils. Tiny scythes of garlic, a red bloom of tomato. Marcel rose quickly, the chair grated, brought back an omelette on a large, smoking dish. It looked very good. It smelled of spices and melted cheese and eggs and made the *avocat's* stomach rumble. A light steam rose from it, it wobbled, alive. Marcel slices, dishes, wonderful green stalks of this and delicious yellow daubs of that showed in the belly of the omelette. He found that he could swallow without the least difficulty. The food settled him.

"What's the magazine?"

Marcel held it up to him. The cover was a fat man riding, or sliding, on the back of a motorbike, and round his neck alarmed animals clung with frightened expressions on their faces. The headline bleated **Fontaine et Easy-Rider.**

"*Le Magazine Littéraire.* The very best. France is *still* the centre of the literary world. It is a privilege . . . ."

"Hmm," went the *avocat*, like a little wind-up toy. The omelette was very good, a glissando of oil, a chunky onion, a slather of moist bacon, the *avocat* thought of music and wondered what the concert would be like, the wine soothed him, the food lulled him, perhaps the world was not so bad. A sharp spine of herb was stuck between his teeth, he worked his tongue into contortions trying to prise it loose. Perhaps also, he thought, the doctor will tell me I have only so long to live. Marcel will go for a blood-test out of guilt, then. *Séropositif.* Ah, verdict of verdicts! He will die of guilt.

"Well, I'll be in it, one day."

"You may indeed."

"You're nobody until they've interviewed you, you know. Of course, you can create yourself, if you wish. That's the way it works. But we take our literature *seriously*. One review is all it takes; then, well....."

"Ah," chided the *avocat* maliciously, aware suddenly of his capacity for spite. "You've become quite the man of letters, Marcel. Quite the well-read man. I applaud you."

The *avocat* raised his glass. Red wine washed its curves, the light through the glass was magnificent, like sunlight through a window at Chartres. Perhaps there is an afterlife, the *avocat* thought.

Grudgingly, Marcel raised his glass. A tink, a punctuative sound.

"You taught me to read *properly*. I owe you that. You showed me *real* books. It was one of the things I most admired in you, that ability to offer yourself, not just the books, the things you knew, but..., well, so unselfishly."

Marcel's voice had dropped a tone or two. The Queen had disappeared back into her deck of cards. Was this now the Joker? Was Marcel a parcel of masks? Or was this what love looked like when one looked at oneself through the eyes of a mask?

"The pupil out-learns the master. Now you are the poet, I am still the poor man at law. I will never write a line, a verse. Think of it! The things I've seen, you'd imagine I'd have stories to write, any amount of material. But no. There is nothing poetic in my working life. Nothing lyrical cries out of the dungeons."

The *avocat* saw the shape of his moroseness gathering like pestilential smoke over the table, shifted from it, shoved it away; such poison, like gas, the sting in the closing throat, if he could only think of music, or die in his sleep. He slurped his wine, the sort of thing one should only do with a fat Burgundy. Certain manners, the world of law had taught him. It wasn't poetry, but it would do.

The sound of knives and forks on plates, the rough exchange of bread in its neat woven basket, the drip of red wine onto the table. In the street, the babble of girls' voices as they went past the window. Marcel continued reading, dreaming of his own face looking back at him; the *avocat* thought of his own death and of music rising courteously to the dark roof of a chapel in which kings and queens gilded everything with the escutcheons of their earthly pomp and power; where a modest but musically astute crowd would applaud, and perhaps he would know some of them. Coats-of-arms of the great houses of Spain and France would smile down at them indulgently; they were nothing, all was dust. The Revolution had carried away the bones of Christ Himself.

The *avocat* saw himself, as so many times before, mounting the steps into the Palais de Justice, navigating with Marcel − his slave carried back from Louisianna or somewhere − at his side the vast and humbling corridors past the bored security staff who moved deliberately and slowly like figures in a piece of performance art, the dry, enormous doors, under lights that gathered no motes of human dust; down, down, turning this way, then that, past corridors marked for peasant and plaintiff, often one and the same − that other Marcel, by name Étienne, shoving his way towards the bed of the Dauphin Charles himself, dagger aloft, nothing was sacred − as if conspiring together to find and then finding the Sainte-Chapelle, solemn, mute to begin with, almost a glorious and fragile disappointment, even as it if flew madly towards Heaven. How solicitous the organisers of the evening's entertainment! How necessary, those little printed programmes! How gracious the black-suited musicians, memorial and regent the theorbo, silly and childish the tambour, tidy the psaltery, cheeky the haut-bois, the vièlles, how beautiful the girls and men against the altar like priests about a holy commemoration! He felt ridiculously sad again, Marcel leafing with a greasy fingertip the glossed pages of the literary magazine, looking for the shadow of his approaching self; as the *avocat* saw in the mirror of every thought, the reflexion of every feeling, his own ghostly back retreating down the long stone corridors of the Palais, invisible to every thing that lived, watched only by dead kings or pestered by supplicants, pursued, sought after by drunken revellers who would eventually ransack the bones of Christ.

The sound of the lights going out was the noise of something falling off a table, he prepared himself for it, the wind-down of men's shouts, someone singing, a quiet which was restless as a pile of compost full of vermin, the growing light in the cell melancholy, sad, of summers long ago which never happened, a regret without cause rooted in everything; without a watch basically he knew now by instinct what time they shut the lights out and in a few minutes the eyes growing accustomed to the painted dark the light from the window would come in, you could stand up and put your arms a little way through, or one arm anyway, feel the cool breeze, he didn't do it, the prisoners did, a night ritual, like sending out distress flags from a sinking ship.

Now he stood up and found that he could do it, opening the inner pane, and he hung one arm up to his elbow fifty feet above the yard and felt a soothing warm drizzle prickle the surface of his skin, his arm grew tired and sore doing it, he withdrew it, tried the other one, he felt the drizzle on his skin and heard the noise of traffic, horns, engines revving, so far away it came to him like a dream, a jangle of sound constructing images in his head, and with it came a tang, a metallic smell of the bodysweat of cities everywhere, the eye in his door opened and closed again, he didn't care that anyone saw him with one arm ludicrously postured through the bars of his cell, anyway someone laughed at the other side of the door and closed the Judas, the prison was said to be the oldest in Paris, did anyone passing by look up at its walls, see arms like his own like the fleshy detritus of a car-bomb blown high up in the wall and imagine human beings like themselves; he'd masturbated and his fingers smelled, no matter how he washed them, of the salts of his balls, perhaps he hoped the drizzle now would scour them, that some essence of himself would fly away on the wind and impregnate a girl bending over in a field somewhere, or opening her legs for a man in an alleyway, it didn't matter, he had the odd imagining that nothing of himself, or of anyone else for that matter, left anything behind, that every molecule was destroyed, swept away, even those of memory, and nothing remained, not even a myth of a person; men laughed and shouted in the street, so near, so far, and the light of the warm moist evening gradually filtered into the cell, washing it with a vague blue, somewhere there was a sun beginning to go down into an endless sea, hissing as it dissolved like a great glowing aspirin tablet in the bowl of the ocean, he left his arm there until it was numb, then drew it in, left the inside window open, the breeze was cooling, he smoked.

He waited for a moment and then took up the letter again, the fatuous stamp of the prison on the envelope, they'd opened it, of course, only to be expected, regulations, no privacy here, and by the gentle light suffusing the cell he read what she had to say, the feel and – he imagined – the definite scent of the paper reminding him loosely of her, though he had trouble getting a clear remembrance of her face, they had all been one person, after all, united, body and soul, man and woman, in the absoluteness of their quest, mission, call it what you will; the imagined scent of all of that was in the paper, he fondled the single sheet. Handwritten, a hundred words or less, but enough to choke him; no one remembered, not really, it had come as a brief, exhilarating shock, like an unsatisfactory orgasm and afterwards there was their embarrassment at realising he had given more of himself than any of them, in the end, but not for the right reasons, no, he hadn't fallen in the line of duty, as it were, it was an act of betrayal, they had decided but that wasn't in the letter. The address might have been the location of a crater on the moon: *I enclose a clipping from a Sunday paper, it doesn't matter which, it's a rag, they're all the same, owned by Corporates. No free media anymore Ha-Ha! Look at how they described you, I never knew you were that age, twice as old as some of them at Shannon that time. There's no one doing anything there now. Not much anyway, the camp is gone, Yanks have tank-busters on the runway, or is it the apron??? And there's a trial coming up, Paddys all taking it up the hole from Amerikay....*

He smiled again at that, he knew the trial, an important trial, a relevant trial, *not like yours*, the words whispered amongst themselves, little diplomats. The piece in the Sunday paper was three paragraphs long, and each paragraph ran to three lines. The heading – it had obviously been a side-bar story, one of those distinguished by their spidery typeface, by their lack of general interest, localised interest, to readers – was maddeningly simple and direct, like an ancient advertisement for liver pills:

Irishman
Held
Over Paris
Murder

Above the headline, where the piece had been cut – hacked? – roughly and without much love out of the newspaper, ran the ragged remnants of a caption to a photograph; he read this over and over, trying to conjure up the photo, the subjects:

...irlfriend of W lli   d ist f Me   n t   ing –

and the enigma, the indecipherable code had at first occupied all of his attention, he couldn't be bothered to read the rest of the letter, its platitudinous tone, the wish-you-were-here-but-not-just-yet voice under every other possible voice, the wound in the letter, yet the immensity of the thought that somehow they'd found out where he was, someone had taken that much trouble at least, deciding to write because making decisions was always difficult, always had been for all of them, for all their marching they were not direct action people, they were more like dreams trying to crowd inside the same short spasm of sleep, like captions without pictures, and he should reply, he should make it his business to reply, they had been so conscientious about writing to Irishmen imprisoned rightly or wrongly in Far Eastern jails, inspired by the implied squalor, disease, failure, the mystical link between understanding and suffering; now they had written to him, he knew he should have suffered more, being *held* carried none of the glorious symbolism of losing one's health in a tubercular hole in an exotic land, he should write back and tell them that he was sorry he couldn't offer them the sacrament of deeper suffering, be a Christ for Christ's sake, a round wafer of a man on a plate for them, they could swallow him, ingest his horror, draw a placard with his face on it and become part of his body for the length of time it took them to walk the length of a street, chanting, hymning his name, and all he was was *held*, the details in the piece scrappy, here and there it seemed he could detect a minute sliver of wood from the pulp pushing up, like the fin of a miniscule shark, through the white water of the newsprint, police, yes, were looking, yes, for a girl and yes it was murder, stabbed, found at the bottom of a flight of stairs; there was always the possibility, the suggestion, of illicitness, a sweet illegality, in the circumstances of his living – and was Paris as exotic as they said?

In spite of himself, the letter and the newspaper item had the effect of restoring him, the words of his dainty little lawyer had clung like parasites, nipped at him, drained his blood, sapped his energy, they would undoubtedly find the girl, only a pearl of a hope that they wouldn't, and she'd say what she had to say. Did it matter?

He had watched her crossing the courtyard, the night had been suddenly cold as if the stars had gone out, he had remained seated on the demolished, wrecked floor of the painter's studio, every eye in every portrait watching him, the smell of himself mingling with the smells of cigarette smoke and alcohol and thinners and paint, nothing left to do, the painter and the girl, once they'd left the room, had donated to it an emptiness and loneliness he could never have imagined possible in the world, a hole into which he'd fallen, or thrown himself, he had taken two Valium, swallowed them down with more canned cheap beer, begun talking to himself about this and that, creating fantasies so delicious he could taste them on his tongue, creamy dreams of fuckable girls, of spread legs, of faces contorted beneath him, mad imaginings – nothing revolutionary, no drunk dreams of revising the entire world – he had let them roll on and then had come the crying-dreams, *snuff-sniffle-sniff*, tight balls of sadness, lovely, delicious, mouthwatering regret, he had listened to some music, not understanding or even making out a single word, embracing the self-disgust at the centre of this wet gratifying lovely maudlinity, wishing to die and seeing her standing over his coffin in tears, a plaque to him on the wall of this room, fuck the painter; he would stamp his hot mark on Paris, he would be unforgettable in his demise, the walls began to move, he threw up, splattered a slimy green liquid all over the carpet, the painter would go insane but fuck him, now there was another smell in the room, did smells have colours? Shivering, nerve-ends flashing, sputtering, the walls vibrated, the paintings leered, he struck one of them with his fist and his hand went straight through the canvas, ragged tongues, deadly, skin-textured, licked around his arm, a whole face obliterated by one blow, at his wrist was the gate of a castle, the edges of the smashed canvas tickled his skin, at his toe was a winding river and sheep grazed on its banks, this was the end the utter wipeout no coming back or forgiveness there were some things you just could not must not do; he was dizzy and angry, only one real noise in the world now; the painter shouting he kicked old papers beer cans paintings out of the way went out into the yard cold old flagstones ancient Paris in gritty crumbs under the soles of his shoes and below the Roman vaults over them again the wet cobbles *Paname*; Vatel had run himself through because the fish ran out, too many cooks, where had he read that? *ya drunken fucker* slipping on the rubbish of the yard, wood, nails, rust, papers, rat-scuffle, drain-tinkle, the painter's voice like the voice of God roaring the yard into existence; and the slum tumbrils crones knitting heads will roll *Allons!* a 'plane's nudge in the heights of flattening sky the light descending from it, please George Dubbya don't bomb Paris! whoever is with me is against me granddaddy dollar-dealing with Hitler access of evil a moon pocket-sized wafer on the plate of the heavens or is it pennies for the black babies? face cooling in the breeze clatter of a rat a cat someone high above his head shouting a window opening sharp as a razor *ugghh!* the painter *grunt-grunt* saying something rings like bullets that scar pulsing trying to climb away from his nose he imagined under the man's fat belly a flapping cock the size of child's thumb his hands on the girl's cunt he tasted the leftover acid from his spewing up whimpering idiot, piss-artist, and a *slap-slap* you won't *fuckingwell* treat her like that *Silence, petits oiseaux* he was at the bottom of the steps a new energy clarity he could see the future ancient worlds this is what it is like to be at the raging centre which cannot hold of things wood-on-wood sounds as if trees fell against each other in Dante's forest of consciousness for guilt have I none; the pheasants are rebolting, he made hard grabs at the air and a wooden banister appears in his fist Jacob's ladder to climb the angels up and down *in aeternam gloriam* nothing could harm him Saint Denis walked a hundred paces carrying his head in his hands I'll plant his head in his hands for him the heavy steps of the painter he put his foot on the first step – what would he find at the top of the stairs, at the child's dark there, menacing, seducing, the shadow through which all other shadows merge and flow, as if he were on not a set of steps but a sort of escalator, once boarded he moved whether he wished to or not?

Heart whack-whacking like a caged bird trying to get out. A few steps up he could see over the wall into the street. Empty, yellow-lit. Then the 'bus-shelter, the poster under plastic saying every man was entitled to a roof over his head.

A long white streak where a knife had drawn its sharp lick along it lovingly, going deep.

In a passion of turbulent light she found the bridge, or it found her, a continuation natural as breathing of every step she had already taken and the beginning of every step she would take in the future, crossed it, the brilliance of the seething *'mouche* searchlights – were they searching for her? – scouring her eyes.

She was hungry, what she'd managed to buy didn't take away the hunger, she turned her mind back into the old way of thinking, like turning a paper bag inside out, planning, creating maps of a city invisible to the people who rushed by, their mouths, lips working furiously, as if a great endless argument were taking place, leaving trails of perfume and scent behind them like smoke from falling, burning objects; she wanted to sleep, and comfortably, she yearned for the disinterested embrace of blankets, she remembered the barge that you could sleep on, stay there, if you knew where it was, it floated behind her eyes as if it sailed in the sky, just out of reach; there was a map too, if she could find it, which would bring her to a *camion,* and the tang, intoxicating, of hot food would scratch her senses, bring saliva into her dry mouth, long before the vehicle appeared, glistening, glowing, almost beyond their expectations, a dole of food making her, them, whole again, charging the depleted heart, creating sleep and dreams, the *camions* were chariots driven by saints.

In a world of saints and barges that cried a welcome from the sky on the roof of her head there were small wakings of men and women, lines of figures without substance, invisible – like sketches on his wall, rip-outs of sketches, by the Dutchman, what was his name? – rising from their warm Métro grilles, slow as figures in a dream or a dance, almost erotic in their slowness, as if they had all the time in the world, arriving at the *camion,* sensing the approaching food by instinct, a gift resurfacing through all the gifts of civilisation, so that they could survive, this army peeling itself from walls, porticoes, even the pillars of the mighty – and utterly irrelevant – Opéra, forgetting for the moment the cardboard squares which they hung around their necks, *J'ai faim, J'ai faim*; Haussman's majestic Opéra that hurled arias over their lice-rich scalps, reciting their own wordless, tuneless songs, moving along the boulevard des Capucines or down the blazing avenue de l'Opéra like lazars, how quickly – and with what disgust and terror! – people made space for them, quickening a step here and there, scuttling like malignant crabs, carapaced, dripping, almost blind, past the fire of lights and the gallant occupied cigarette-smoke-in-the-warm-street-air tables of the Café de la Paix; then some going in another direction, lost or not lost, sensing something else, panicked in the Chaussée d'Antin, as if they'd drifted to the surface of another planet, no one ever challenged the immense and unreachable stars of the place Vendôme, where, it was known, you could evaporate in the gold-dense oxygen, bad enough the confusion of the place de l'Opéra, those whirling, ever-moving bodies of red, white, green, blue light, traffic unending, without direction, comets of steel, asteroids of flesh, the same cars and taxis and people round and round forever, as if under a curse; a city moving within a city, parallel to it but never touching it, without age, history, geography, a sense of time, without a language or commerce or constitution, death being in life here more than any priest could ever clamour on about; her body under someone – when? – its whimpers, his, like those of a kicked dog even as he came there was never in his eyes a man's shine of victory, sometimes she did it to keep warm. The taxis primped by like butterflies. The giddy eyes of young girls were unnaturally beautiful.

In a spurt of chemical energy she would take a step or two and skip as she'd done so often, *Lulu-Lulu,* when she was a very small child, something to fit into the palm of a grown-up's hand, a flitter of images now even as her feet left the smooth curve of the surface of the bridge, so quickly she could not hold on to any one of them, a balcony, a woman's face not unkind, the prickle of hot sun, a pixie of a girl she had been, *able to fit into the palm of a grown-up's hand.* She felt the weight of everything she was carrying haul her back down to the ground, she might dissolve through the metal and concrete and vanish into the river, walking on a bridge was like being suspended between heaven and earth, it was like being an angel steadying her wings to take flight over the city.

But she was not there, thank God, she was somewhere else arrived from somewhere else equally uncharted, a galaxy which spun about its core a million-million other places, even as the door opens and he's standing there, the painter is ripping her hair out of her scalp, and there is a look on his face which tells her in an instant that he is helpless, powerless, no rescuer he, no white horse under him, the painter shaking her, words spitting into her eyes, her nose, she's already naked, it started when she was naked, she can't remember why, perhaps nakedness infuriated the painter, its frankness, its lack of reason; she was over the bridge, not skipping now, it wasn't polite to make a show in public.

Police vehicles, the unhurried sway of the *police urbaine*, like little girls shy amongst the adults, lights knock-knocking against the blue air, she balanced herself on the edge of the kerb, her nostrils tickled, teased, by a faint whiff − a distant chemical fire − sharp, of her own blood and other deep fluids pulsing between her legs, a tall Black woman, like a shaft of a tree carved, preciously, to look like a woman, moved in beside her then moved away, diamonds of light breaking on the ebony black of her tiny handbag, eyes straight ahead, as the lights changed; mopeds, big motorcycles, cars whose roofs were flying carpets of street lights, café lights, the nearness of many people, their bodies touching, untouching, as their voices did not touch or untouch her ears, she crossed the street breathing in the thick stale warmth of diesel and petrol fumes, she would eat soon, the hunger was like small insatiable animals gnawing under the drumhead of her belly. A *SAMU* bent itself through the traffic, horn hysterical, lights going off and on in the windows of closed shops.

She had the feeling that she was swimming, that the city was under water; the air thickened. She could see him in front of her, the young man, leaning out, reaching out, as if to stop her falling. Her hands were sticky and she licked her fingers without meaning to do so, the reaction of a child, taste like the taste of an iron railing. The young man was very pale in the scattery light of the yard.

She didn't want those images. She lowered her head, shaking it from side to side vigorously, someone going by swore at her. She swam in the air now, in and out the arches of an arcade, happier in the shadows, the arches like eyelids raised in surprise, the air full of the scent of water and salt. An elderly woman brushed against her, a touch as alien as if the woman had been a tree. Her hunger had been replaced by a curious delight in the emptiness inside her body, the vacancy of it; her mother's tears, meaningless and insincere, while the suction plucked a bloody red thing like a small beef sausage from her insides and then her mother's rage, thumping at her even as she lay under the thick white bedclothes; just another image, she could see these pictures and feel nothing, as if she were seeing into the thoughts of someone else, a stranger. Trees and children laughing and the smell of old woman, a patience in the air and a glass of sunny lemonade. A dream.

Rising up in front of her now, an angel, declaring herself in honey-runny light above the rue Sainte-Honoré; distant but distinctive, she squinted to see her, this angel with her petard aloft, she seemed to emerge from the caverns of great, thunderous buildings, the black wingfolds of busy and terrifying architecture. Garlands of diamonds of light hung in the galleries of the rue de Rivoli, but no matter, such baubles were of no consequence; this angel-light was sacramental, shimmering, like golden smoke it drew her on, she wanted to inhale its sweet warmth, transmuting into gold herself.

Proud, shining, reflecting, absorbing every light in the city, every gleam and sparkle, flying in the underwater air, golden on a golden horse, the angel pranced nearer, a girl with a raised standard over her, all she had to do was leap on the back of the horse, get on behind her, this armoured girl so beautiful that she had drained the sun itself of its colour, she ran to her, blood warm between her thighs, warm and sticky and smelling of herself, knowing the girl would clean her up, feed her, take her above the city to the soft indifference of clouds; the girl on the horse had come from nowhere, a miracle, suddenly she had been there, a creature of womanly fire in the middle of an ocean of concrete and stone, she ran faster now, the girl on the horse growing larger and larger, the light from the horse's flanks brighter and brighter and the gold gleaming on the girl's breast, molten and warm, simmering, protecting a golden heart; the comfort she offered! And as she reached out for it, the girl on the horse rising above her now, slowly, slowly, the muscles in the legs of the horse glittering and twitching and full of amazing light, the girl looked down at her, smiled or laughed, it was difficult to tell when the hooves of the great glittering horse smashed down, those impetuous, unstoppable hooves caressing her, breaking her, clawing down inside her. She felt luxuriously tired under the legs of the horse, happily she could have allowed him to pound her forever into the Paris street, below the street, into the catacombs, the yellow Parisian earth; her mother weeping, her face ugly in tears, a memory, the blood on the white sheet from where the child had been ripped from her, a small brown island, a continent an inch across on the white empty space of the bed.

In the liquid folding darkness she felt exquisitely happy.

The Third Day

Someone had thrown sugar in his eyes. Or sand. Perhaps Marcel had done it, prised his eyelids apart while he slept and poured a gritty substance under them, perhaps Marcel wanted him blind on top of everything else.

It was very early in the morning, his head was an ancient and decorated roomful of music, and the royalty of France and Spain hung out engraved and painted ornaments, along with their sovereign angels, from the intricate friezes of the chapel ceiling. The music sublime, he had escaped himself. The viols had a dark wood-thick timbre behind the sharp hysteria of a psaltery; a conversation in music, a miracle drawn out of the well of an imagination four hundred years old. Marcel had fallen asleep and snored. But what of it.

In the wee hours of the morning, a time neither dark nor light, the *avocat* woke from a dream of buying roasted chestnuts from a vendor at his brazier on the rue de Rivoli; it was almost Christmas, snowing, lights everywhere. Bells rang and buzzed; out of the dream he reached for his bedside telephone. Marcel's black form against the snow-white single sheet was like an unreachable range of mountains in the distance of some unknowable country. There was not a sound in the street, in the whole world, save for the belling of his 'phone.

"I would not have called if it were not so important, Hervé."

Marie, at this hour, thinking of his welfare. Did she have a life of her own? A personal, sweaty life, where she groaned, moaned, even washed dishes and got drunk? Agitated, his voice thick with the aftertaste of Marcel's cock and the red bite of late night wine, he tried to make a suitable reply, one that would not be rude to the sleeping world.

"Marie. You are too good to me."

"I could be kinder, but all God allows me is to flirt with you. God's queer, like you. The big lawyer now, Hervé. No longer the little village *avocaillon*."

He sat up on one elbow. Her voice was slurred, her little jibe carried no weight and besides, she would never insult him. No longer the village lawyer; perhaps she *was* insulting him. Perhaps he didn't know her after all; what was there to know in any case? People were people, the shapes of their lives were not imaginable to others, even to themselves. Take, for instance, the shape *his* life assumed when jammed into the matrix made by himself and Marcel.

"God should be in prison. What's up?"

"They've found the girl, she thought Joan of Arc was coming down off her statue, or maybe she thought *she* was Joan of Arc. Anyway, she wasn't well received either way; a car hit her and knocked her off her pedestal."

"I'm not sure I...... "

"You know where the damned statue is, Hervé. She was running across the street, arms outstretched, stoned no doubt, and that was that. *Clac!*"

The *avocat* thought he heard her lips slip wetly across the rim of a glass, the tip of her tongue grating off her palate to make that last silly sound; alone, but busy, a sense of having something to do, even as the clocks of the world moved steadily on into the worst and loneliest darks of the night. He wondered whether Marie, like so many, would choose such a time to walk in the Seine; a normal day, she'd lock up, go home; on the other hand, black thoughts could come to anyone. He was having them now.

154

"Stay there."

He got up – did Marcel, that range of muscular mountains, move? – and padded into the bathroom, opened a cabinet, rattled a box, took out a low dose Tranxene, swallowed it, went back into the dark and smelly bedroom; love had been made there, violent, noisy, wet, slurpy as an ice-cream cone; and as cold. The drug would take the grittiness out of his eyes, let him think; Marcel turned over more obviously now, grunted, dreamed of God only knew what.

"I'm back."

"Do you want me to meet you at the office? I can be ready in half an hour?"

Yes, he thought, of course you can. Mouthwash, a little make-up; a beautiful woman, a real woman, some man should have taken her a long time ago; but how did he know some man did not grumble and turn over in her bed even as they spoke? What was the sense in considering the value of others' lives like this? Night thoughts, anxieties given strange forms: Marcel's cock had become almost invisible in the dark and there was, without a doubt, something obscene and unacceptable about having a lover's sausagy cock in your mouth an hour after you'd been treated to something by Monteverdi.

He knew that other telephones were ringing in various bedrooms in Paris, just as his had, the 'phones of magistrates, policemen, journalists. Piaf's city constantly rehearsing small tragedies, singing about them, infidelities and letdowns like an injection of vitamins to the vein; irresistible. New energy stirred everything.

Now everyone reacted with the mock-urgency of players suddenly called on stage to play their parts, rehearsed to the last degree, dressing, arranging make-up even as the shutters slammed up – the city was a marvellous theatre, a stage, a backdrop, songs – on early shops and market-stalls grew vegetables, fish, fruit, meat, confectionery, clothing, items of dubious interest, from the Marché aux Puces to the gates of the city at Nation.

As if great wheels under the city lurched, moved, gears connecting, little dolls above ground in their thousands beginning to move and whirl, toy vehicles cranking forward.....

"Have you dozed off on me? What has your little chocolate auntie being doing to you?"

"Let it fall, you. You're being vulgar, Marie. You have my undying gratitude for this call. "

"I'm halfway down a bottle. You know nothing about me."

"Okay. I will bring you flowers, I promise you. Now have you made a list?"

"I don't want your fucking flowers. Do you intend to go and see the girl? She's badly banged up, but then I'd say she's been banged up in one sense or another all her life. *Vive les ados!* She's a street-kid, Hervé; they tell me she's about fourteen."

"I doubt she's that young. Though it could be her selling point. I will see her. But I think really I should go and see my client. Then I'm going to see my mother. What are the cops saying, our magistrate?"

Marie dutifully called off a brief table of names, who was doing what, what opinions were being held, who had moved in for an interview, what her studious, if tipsy, inquiries had revealed for him.

"She killed him, Hervé. It took her two seconds out of her drug kick and she was scratching it on the walls, according to what I hear, but the walls were making copies. Everyone was there, naturally. Even Saloman's flunkies. You'll need to see him, by the way. Your client's a fool. The tale she had to tell!"

The *avocat* looked at Marcel's shining back. He could smother him now, stab him; murder was not as complicated, not the big deal, it was made out to be. Breaking into a house was more difficult, required much more planning and rehearsing. Marie's voice undulated like the ripples of a meek and self-obsessed river.

156

"He sees himself as a hero. He sees himself, rather, as Jesus Christ or someone, sacrificing himself for our sins. Who knows?"

For a breath or two, Marie said nothing. Was she weeping? It seemed so. He could hear her sniffling, not a head cold, something more serious. Then the slippery sipping sounds again.

"Such garbage, Hervé! I wanted to be a nun when I was a child," Marie said. Oh, her voice was intolerably, irredeemably sad. Her voice was a vacuum, it sucked every other possible sound into it, it sucked at his ear.

"Get some sleep, Marie. You've earned it."

"Come and lie beside me, Hervé."

"Good night, Marie. God bless."

"*Chou.* Now you're a fucking priest!"

"You'll regret all of this in the morning."

"It is my destiny, *Maître*."

He replaced the receiver as quietly – that is to say, as gently in the emotional sense – as he physically could. Marcel was up and sitting on the edge of the bed. The ridges of his spine looked hard and knuckly as tumours. Once, the *avocat*, sitting in a barber's chair, had been able – the barber was so close, so physical, for God's sake – to sniff the very odours of the man's body and read them as if they were words on a page of skin; sweat, the tart sting of something else, an aftershave perhaps; above all, he could smell faintly but unmistakably that the man had made love not so long ago, from his arms the foreign stain of another's body, from his crotch, though so faintly that only an emotional detective such as himself could pick it up, a paranoiac who feared and loved at the same time, the lustrous sharp nail-scrape scent of semen that hadn't quite dried and hardened and the man had been in a hurry, late for work, who knew what, and there'd been no time for a quick wash-down, a splash of *Bien-être*, or he'd forgotten, regretted it on the 'bus but couldn't rectify the situation, hadn't time, hoped to have time

157

when he clocked in, but it hadn't been possible, no, the scent remained and along with it the knowledge that all lovers had, that the spoor of their lovemaking remained with them in some secret place which nevertheless would reveal itself to total strangers at the most awkward moments and in the least delicate situations when, for instance, your job could be on the line if someone took offence; the man had done a very good job on his hair, spruced him up very nicely indeed, sprayed something discreet on his scalp, the *avocat* had gone out into the Paris sun feeling very good about himself, saw his reflection in a shop window, liked the image – the professional man, competent, groomed, not afraid to use some *sérum visage* to keep the wrinkles at bay – and strolled off towards the Palais or perhaps that big gloomy very public office, one place merged into the other so often, and perhaps that day Marie had flirted again with him, her lithe legs resting themselves on the edge of his desk, every man in the place wanting her and she wanting only the queer; and not because, as with some women, because he was *safe*, no, quite the opposite. She wanted to fuck him. Now what kind of justice was that?

And when he tried to recall to his nostrils – it is true that memory in the form of smell lives on forever in the nose – the barber, that betraying musk, the one that mattered, he could not. It was gone.

It was not, after all, that memorable. Intimate smells were everywhere, you only had to be ready to receive them; Marie too had her smells, warm, deep scents nothing artificial could obscure. Sometimes, on some strange days when it was peculiarly warm in the office in spite of its size, he could pick them up as she passed him, or stood close enough to him; Marie's smell in those moments was dark and earthy, tangy too, a drift, sudden and disappearing in a blink of an eye; oddly – he could not explain this to himself, so why try? – the scent made him want to reach out and touch her, for the briefest of moments, on the shoulder. Just that, nothing more.

158

He shaved, dressed himself. Marcel made coffee, made coffee for both of them.

"Who was that?"

"Work. There's been a break, you know how it is."

He hated Marcel in that moment, he wished not to have to explain anything about himself to anybody. He was himself. He was doing his duty. No one could intrude upon that – the very insolence of it! *Go back to your bar, your girly-boy waiters and your fuck-cooks!*

Fuck-cooks – there was an amusing expression.

He telephoned for a taxi.

Marcel looked helpless all of a sudden, a naked child, not knowing what to do, the next precise thing. The *avocat* lunged at him awkwardly, certainly not tenderly, and kissed him on the mouth.

"I'll be back, then I'm taking the car and driving up to my mother."

"Do you want me to be here when you come back?"

"That's up to you. Are we reaching a delicate point? I can't explain it."

"You think I'm unfaithful."

"In some ways, it doesn't matter whether you are or not. I know I'm curious, a bit anxious, but that's not the same thing. Let's not discuss it now. I can't think of it now."

Marcel close to tears; this was not a good way to part in the morning. But the world didn't make such naïve allowances.

The *avocat* closed the door behind him. He hoped he had washed away every last trace of love making and the body of another man. He wanted to enter the new born morning world as if he himself had just been born. He carried secret news. His *portable* whined, an irritating piece of Beethoven he'd meant to change; he looked at the number. Herbuterne. The world wanted him.

He stood rigidly on the pavement in the lightening dark and watched for his taxi.

The corridors were cylindrical drums pounding over and over, the same mental note; voices, orders then, laughter, bleak defiance; a stick prattled against a rail, figures lurched into yellow prison light, strips that flickered in the walls like alien creatures dying or signalling to each other, naked orbs, behind steel mesh; a bell – a discordantly holy sound – he shat and wiped himself, the smell was acidic and brutal and did not move and all around him – he could sense these patterns now, knew their nature – men in a ridiculous guarded privacy did the same. His door opened: a command, he stepped out and joined a rustling, muttering queue, more commands – did it matter what the words meant? Did one think in terms of signifiers in a place like this? – and he saw, as he always saw, that some men had eyes red from weeping and others had eyes that did not or could not blink; breakfast, a surprisingly wide choice, even as a fat bald man with a swastika tattoo on his arm masturbated under the long table to which some men were chained; the smell was a chemical compound of paint, antiseptic and school food, and a thin man with rodent's eyes and no teeth cheeped like a small animal directly across from him as he sat with his moulded plastic tray, started in with drugged determination – they gave him something every night, and the sleep kept away thoughts of being hemmed in and of the real world beyond his window; he had picked up more slang, more street argot by the passing hour, the minute, and he was conscious of not being the same man, or of being a completely different man, from the one who had walked with the girl, argued art and politics with the painter, such things were pointless dreams, speculations on another life and it was best not to entertain them; names were called over a rusting microphone and fed in staccato bursts around the room, already loud with fraying nerves and men trying to eat; *La guernon,* for that was the skinny man's name in here, he had been christened thus because it was said that he cheeped as loud as a monkey when he took it from behind, had stabbed a male prostitute in the anus with the neck of a broken bottle and watched while the man had bled to death, laughed at something, nodded to him and then down at the fat man, whose right arm was increasing its pace, his face growing redder; and he heard his name called out, barely, but he heard it, and thought with a tang of bitterness of his tiny useless lawyer who would visit him with more questions and a distance that he found moving and at the same time intolerable, as if the little man were afraid of him, *a shadow,* as the others called him, not a real prisoner in the strict sense because they were all condemned and had no hope and looked for none, he was still in with a chance, the little nervous lawyer represented that and they resented him for those visits but here came another one; the letters from his own embassy were frequent but unashamedly brusque and official, as if he were a shadow even in their eyes, a name, a number in a filing cabinet, a filed embarrassment; still, even eating, he could see her, the girl, and the shape in which he had left the painter, their two faces melding often, becoming one, and he owned her because he was a sharer, an accomplice, in her very history and even the tranquillisers could not take her away, though they tried; he kept her face hidden under the folds of his diminished heart, whether she was alive or dead was irrelevant, the past began with the banging of the corridors, much as the future did, there was nothing – it had taken him a few days, but he understood now that the fear had subsided – that could make the space and time he moved through in here coincide in the least way with time and space as it was understood by human beings on the outside, the streets, the cafés, even in the empty spaces occupied by ghosts of the revolutions he had planned with those phantasms, grim and ugly in their posturing, or so they all seemed now, who belonged to a past remoter still; like lives imagined of strange creatures on another planet from whom vague and unintelligible static sometimes squeaked through; not even the language of the country of his imprisonment was much spoken in here, there was another language, a code if you like, which, once learned or even scrappily grasped, became your language more utterly than any other you had once spoken; a man was a female monkey, for example, and he was a shadow.

Meanwhile the fat masturbating man had fulfilled himself and was buttering some toast with the delicacy of a child paraded in front of approving neighbours.

Hierarchies – like those of the angels, perhaps? – gangs and tribes and leaders of tribes; the world outside mirrored itself murkily here, there was corruption, sex for sale, and even privileges bought with cigarettes, lighters, one's own body; nothing unusual, in other words, thrived in this metal and cement world that hadn't its counterpart and its cultivating dish in the world over the walls, beyond the rolls of wire, through the lines of trees – the miracles he could occasionally see! – and even as, after a passing of what seemed like only a handful of hours he could tell that his cell itself had an identity, an architecture, right down to the blue cloth of the mattress, the yellow paint of the walls, the egg-yolk light in the ceiling, a small table, though he seldom sat at it, and a certain, indefinable *brightness* to it which was quite pleasant when the sun reached in through the window; even to the initials clawed, scraped, knifed into the metal legs of the bed, spelling out the identities, indecipherable to the rest of the world forever, of men who had waited and waited for judgement before him or wept at its cancerous certainty; he had not noticed these things at first, no, too removed into his distress and quite naturally so, who would deny a man his distress?

But he wondered what he would or would not feel, see, think, or hear of this place were he to spend twenty years in it, life lived between footfalls and cracking keys in locks, even the warders growing old, sick, retiring, moving on, everything moving but him, not even death catching him; he looked up from his plastic tray at the red paint of the railings running around the room, the grey walls and the odd but not haphazard

162

walkways, designed to cross and recross each other, as if they were being knitted constantly by some giant hand, the whole a pattern viewable only from heaven; there were round towers, he had seen them, ancient as myths, reaching up with gradual force of alchemical numbers – who knew what went on? – to triangulated roofs on which stately flags flew or antennae hummed, just as there was a wall – let's forget the once-public nature of death by guillotine, or even the privacy, the death-house intimacy of it, a refinement – against which a man was made to stand, a rough canvas hood draped over his head, twenty paces no more no less to the greasy muzzles of six rifles; the stone, the blocky infinite stone, turned black in rain, of everything on the outside, even the surface against which the dead man's blood ran; now there were recreation-rooms and TV rooms and a space for *boules* although a silver shining boule could be wrapped in a cloth or sock and used to crush a skull and the blue sky was there most days when, the warders in bright blue short-sleeved shirts standing on the walls, nothing behind them but wire, sharp as ice, they'd take to the sports field; he wouldn't but *they*, the affirmed, the utterly doomed, would, those who were not shadows but cast shadows, often very thin ones, on the rough red gritty ground.

He heard his name again and stood up, shouted – it was just a sound, all sounds are, essentially, the same sound and he assumed that, just as he had difficulty understanding his name when the warder spoke it, so the warder would have difficulty understanding a reply in his rudimentary French – and the warder was beckoning to him; he joined a queue, the lady-monkey cheeped and from the kitchens as he passed their open doors, all that polished silver, the dull metal, the enormous ranges, the pots cleaned and scrubbed, men in medical whites moving around, singing, making a great importance of being cooks in prison, the rooms and their floors gleaming with the back-work of punishment duty; the queue said nothing because, in those odd few moments between being called and discovering the *reason*

163

for being called, there was nothing to say and it could end in anything, a visit from a lover or a note from her lawyer, even a further accusation, there was no way of knowing, there was no reprieve from the queue; men moved this way and that, and he moved, a thick-fingered hand on his upper arm, into the familiar little room that stank of cigarettes and bad breath and unwashed teeth. To the little froggie lawyer, useless as sticking-plaster on an amputated limb, smiling like a man after the right kind of sex with a beautiful woman – he had seen the morning sun on the pavements too, he had a thousand rights to smile – handing him cigarettes, *Bleues*, then clapping his hands, more sleep wetly unused in them than he had ever imagined possible in a human being's eyes, the man was exhausted from the inside out; he was impatient, and he said what he had to say and then sat back, his hands still clasped, looking at him; then he shook his head, handed him a sheet of paper, everything in French of course, explained it to him carefully, leaned forward, then stood up abruptly as if he had smelled something offensive the more closely he had come. The room's cloying fug of drying paint was now indistinct, distant. *Enjoy your cigarettes*, the lawyer said. *You can buy your own again now, even choose your own brand.*

Rain. Soft, wispy, a snail's slither on the windscreen; the *avocat* driving with finicky care through the glowing, smouldering streets of Paris, traffic heavy, motorcyclists like overgrown bees flitting noisily by, in spite of the mess, the halting and starting, the enormous weight of vehicles of every shape and size somehow the movement continuing, as if the streets moved even when the traffic did not. On his passenger seat, files and a briefcase, a book, Marcel had found it for him at a bookstall years ago, a French hippy writing poems about travelling around America in the 'Sixties – where were *you* in the 'Sixties, *mon brave*? – and on a glanced page the line: "Les empreintes de la vie ont marqué ce visage...." Simplistic, maudlin dross, but Marcel, the trying-to-be-sophisticated half-Arab, was already developing a taste for poetry then, or what passed for it; the red scars on Marcel's cocoa body – who would run their fingers over them in the emptying days descending now?

He was riding on the quai des Tuilleries, the river a silvery green scarf some forgetful god had dropped out of a wrapping tissue of sky. He rolled down a window and the air was full of noises and exhaust fumes; more, the smell of a city waking up from itself, shrugging off dreams and nightmares, pissing itself in lanes. There was a stink to a city that could not be described; warm blood or rotting earth.

Marcel standing in the bedroom door, sleepy and boyish, a ham actor in a role, his considerable *bitte* lolling out of that hairy red patched flesh like a thick stalk on a splattered fruit; reminding him of *La Mouette*, for Christ's sake. As if by recalling his pathetic poetic triumph they could remember simultaneously better times; when strange books didn't appear out of nowhere in the flat and the nudge, no more, of another human being in their lives wasn't palpable on every cup, saucer, door handle, like the groping fingers of a ghost.

Marie early in the office, the young Irishman's voice metallic on the cassette-recorder, questions, replies, packing it away for him; a fussing monument of cheap perfume and hasty mouthwash, preparing him, brisk and efficient, not a word about her lapses on the 'phone – therefore, not a word about her demented loneliness – and the backslaps of a passing colleague, the success of the girl turning up like that, *throwing herself on the mercy of the Maid of Orléans! Quite poetic, don't you think?*

Others would say, as the day progressed that, as the quaint expression had it, Hervé farted higher than his arse, thought he was something, forgot he was a country hick and this was Paris, you couldn't take one accidental success - there was always time, room, for something to go wrong, of course, praise God – and think it meant anything. Over coffee, a marc, the old formula, the cutting-down-to-size.

But he had briefed Herbuterne, called him back, he had been careful but the story was there all the same, the girl was disturbed, abused, the young man was hypnotised by her, thought she could get away, a fool for love: the old hack would know what to do, and how prominently to display his name, story utterly unattributable, Irishman's lawyer had *always known* his client was an innocent man, the curse of *J'Accuse!* Make no mistakes, no diplomatic surges of shit. These old routines danced best; amazed, surprised, frightened by his own actions in calling the journalist, what had he been thinking, only of himself, but there came a time, ambition was no sin, your name in *France Soir*, anywhere at all, but public.

Marcel's ice-cube kiss going out the door; two lovers parting perhaps forever as the train pulls out of the station, black-and-white, the *noir* of love on a white blank screen. There was such lovely wet light in the green mouths of the fishes, dragons, bearded men in bronze on the fountains now, the air greened, it would be a hotter day still, when the haze melted, the spill of rain ceased.

Marie ferrying floats, barges, deep-sea cargoes of correspondence from one desk to another, a formidable woman, good-looking, men inspected her; other work waiting, a decrepit tenement had gone on fire, a dozen Algerians died; a *vendue* most likely Roumanian found throttled near rue Charles Fourier, the rue de Tolbiac end, the whole world probably saw what was going on and kept going, the girl selling herself for the promise of papers, a new world order, what else was new; did anyone want to take up a teenager who'd shouted *Mort aux vaches!* at a motorcycle cop near avenue Pierre Grenier, then ran off into the cemetery? Laughter all round. No one wanted anything as silly as that. Even if the kid had been whacked black and blue. Who'd he think he was, a *rebel?* Laughter. *No more rebels!* Someone punches into the air. Laughter. Good fun. A light morning. He still had poor Jewish Madame Elias and her unsavoury e-mail messages.

Papers in his hands like hard skin, stamped, headed vellum, official, signed with exuberant flourishes, the *palais* of this and that; Marie smiling at him.

"Congratulations, *Maître*."

Formal, forgetting, solid; reliable old Marie. She had on a very formal skirt, too, tweedy, grandmotherish, down to her ankles. Penitential. Sackcloth. For the sins of drunkenness in the small hours of the morning when the world was dutifully abed. Sins of admission.

"Thank you, Marie."

Limp sunlight barring his desk, watery sunlight, not strong yet, give it time; he went into the washroom and saw in the mirror a small man smartly dressed. Faidherbe and ambitious others like him could go fuck themselves. He'd readied himself for the visit to the prison. *Deep breaths.*

He drove now with the radio on, something by *Indochine*, not his usual thing, it kept pace with the motorway speed of his car, he felt so good to be driving, in control, one swerve and lights out. He drove on roads so fast that no shape was solid that was not on a horizon twenty miles away; gasping past two-bodied lorries bound for Italy, Spain, the ancient Orient, so long and big and hardhearted that passing them he could feel their tug, then release, then the bump and jog of fast wind, their clutch on his little vehicle, not that little but it felt so, these bawling animals shouldering and rattling like armies on the move; towards Nemours and never saw that city, towards Auxerre and bypassed it too, as if these towns were decorations – puzzles, mischievous cryptographs – on road-signs, not real places, motorcycle *flics* jackbooted, helmeted, stationed with cameras near the roundabouts; he pulled off the highway and ate a turkey sandwich in a freezingly air-conditioned café space in a service station as big as a *hypermarché,* a bloody great white *souk* of a place with whole families lounging about drinking coffee from plastic cups and Algerians serving; put petrol in his car, had to pay for it in cash because he hadn't – not having used the car for so long – bothered to get a card so that he could just plunge it in to the pay-slot at the pump; he bought chocolates for his mother. He drove past pointers for villages, towns, arrows for magical Avallon, through Bierre, past a place called The White Dog, saw the signs, warnings, turn-offs, *Déviation,* Dijon but he wasn't going there, it had been a thousand years since he had driven down to see her, what had made it so long? Trees, pylons, curious turrets far off, billboards: *Grand Choix – Terrains a Bâtir,* past café-bars with red plastic seats at red tables outside them, empty, ancient wooden doors twice as tall as a man with iron grilles on their slim windows and dulled brass handles like pomegranates or apples going off in the heat tongued by flights of stone steps shiny with footsteps and green thick hard leaves casting shadows over them; rivers still as glass, small boats half submerged as if fused into the water, he drove over the smashed carcasses of dead vermin, he watched the solid white lines and the bone-white smaller lines, he saw the fat green plastic fork indicators coming and going like insects that never quite hit the windscreen; he heard football results and weather forecasts; saw camper-vans measled with stickers, the affordable small adventures adhesively remembered, saw them crowd into lay-bys and slow, slow; saw the reflection of his car in the polished bodies of other vehicles he passed and in the windows of small anxious shops.

He passed those inevitable muttering villages whose only indicator was a thin spire of a church behind Impressionist trees and the trees, thicker here or there, concealment for the wild snuffling boar or the timid, ballet-dancing deer; places lying in ambush, they seemed to him to bear a weight they did not deserve, he was afraid of them, their mysteries and ordinary emptiness, he had felt them follow him; he saw small quiet graveyards, a solitary stone cross in the centre and the date 1871 engraved on its base; a children's area, white-walled graves the size of large shoeboxes, a history of weeping, grief unbearable and inconsolable; of headstones carved with the images of motorcycles, trombones, the flag of France, a football;

the oval portraits, fading and moisture-embossed, smiling faces, young, old, beautiful, plain, clinging like colourful insects to the sturdy marble of the headstones; the dozens of smaller plaques of remembrance from friends, relatives, and the well-meant but crass – to him – verses, a staple of such stones, in which those left behind declared that if tears were flowers the world would be covered in roses, and so forth; the immense silence of these village cemeteries, the silence of the side-by-side churches, doors locked, secrets scuttling in corners, streets hot and empty, as if evacuated; a barber talking football with his one client of the day, crickets sawing amid the graves, distant dog barks, a tractor, invisible over a hot field of green cornstalks the height of a small man; a family tomb, cracking apart in the summery heat; family plots, names joined forever on stone and marble, their myths buried, crumbled, once in such a graveyard with his mother he'd kicked an odd-shaped yellowy stone and it was in fact a section of a spinal column; things coming back up, the earth too dry to support them, the silence, going on forever, the plainchant of unexceptional grief – the uselessness of resisting anything, we all ended up here or somewhere like it; the heat everywhere, our secrets safe. *Bovary – c'est moi!*

The *avocat* – whose name would most certainly be in the papers the next day and with whom Irish legal people would now consult as if he were important – drove on past the villages and felt sorry for them; did they fret, those iron-red roofs, those sand-coloured walls, the silver blue slates of the church tower, when they could, at midnight, take it no more? Did their tears fall on to the hot black streets, mistaken, in the morning, for overnight rain?

Their gutter-fluttering local newspapers ran red with parish tragedies and parlour history: prison farm for a drunk who'd broken up a bar (everyone knew he was *un raté*, a failure); a village had received a government grant to develop a handball alley (why was there no French word for *handball?*); local students photographed doing a research project (fat smiles, young

and old, built squat-arsed, close to the ground); annual pilgrimage
dedicated to the Black Virgin has its dates changed (see le Recteur
père Hubert for details); committee to celebrate the Libération
continues to disagree over number of Jews taken from the village
(a question of what names to put, finally, on the monument, and
who can remember?)

The highways avoided all of it, trawled bigger spaces,
ignored the rural dead and fallen and the grandiose statues in
the paltry squares with those endless lists of young dead of every
war that had ever been, no one left to read them or pray for
them, the highways plundered on.

He sidetracked Beaune, melted into the air and drove
over the limit, faster, faster, to the woman in the hospice bed stiff
as iron unspeaking perhaps unhearing and he would most
definitely see a doctor himself when he got back but oddly he
felt much better as he drove, lighter, as if he could fly, what was
the reason for that; there was Chalon (Nord); here Tournus, there
Macon; the sun blinding him, he puts on sunglasses, the news
on the radio is someone translating the nasal American old-man
tones of Donald Rumsfeld; the fields stretched into the rising
sky, he would sit with her, hold her hand, she would be a doll
awaiting the never-coming kiss of a frog; he didn't know what
time it was, he now felt neither hunger nor fatigue; his *portable*
rang, he ignored it; he stopped again at a station near Fourvière,
then he was in the city of his birth, turning, slowing into traffic
over the rivers, his heart slow, it was almost as if it had stopped
beating; he drove towards the white hospital out towards La
Mulatière, careful now in slower traffic; he parked in the grounds
of the hospice, sat back, closed his eyes. There was little to stop
him simply driving on forever.

A white marbled queen on a tomb, she lay back, his
mother, trapped in this and that tangle of wires, tubes, and the
sounds, alien and monstrous, of machines that sucked and
clicked. Not all of them sucked and clicked for her. Other women,
older by thousands of years, lay preserved in the dark brightness
of the room, and now and then some coughed, which

170

was a form of speech. She looked at him or appeared to; nothing moved. He placed the chocolates on a table beside her bed. A young nurse came in. Departed. He took his mother's hand. It was perhaps just as well that they had nothing to say to each other; neither, for different reasons, could speak. Plastic curtains jiggled and fidgeted over and opened window; the bright corridors smelled of food cooking and airspray and, as always, someone whistled in the distance.

Perhaps they had always been this way, one waiting for the other to crawl back into the other's world – a different world – for just a moment, a second; there was nothing here, no Marcel, no stupid Irishman, no dead painter, street-girl, to remind him of who he was, and yet he knew himself intimately, better than ever, was at ease with himself. He was tired, his emotions were loosening, like diseased bowels; the other old women stirred and moaned, hands brittle and porous as dry leaves on the undisturbed and sinless sheets.

In the hollowed space of their mutual silences, he wept.

An immense freedom, as if the sky itself tugged him upwards, what he felt most was fear, hearing a last lock twisted securely behind him, a casting out, the rituals of abandonment are the same whether being released from jail or from home; they had given him back his possessions but they were not his, nor the clothes he wore, nor his shoes; he had become thinner, lighter, and his breath came at first in fast gulps and his chest tightened. Freedom brought panic and solitude. A hundred yards away a girl cocked her hips beneath a short clinging skirt and he could do no more than glance at her, shy.

A green bus huffed by, faces looked out, neither at him nor away from him, the city going about its business, which was no business of his, a pocketful of small cards the little Peter Sellers lawyer had given him, places to stay, recommended, he saw other prisons smaller and more comfortable and uglier; he saw the impotence of having no identity, for they had not

171

returned his passport and no, he could not leave France or even Paris for that matter, not yet. So the hostels and halfway houses were extensions, nothing more, of the prison that had thrown him out; like a jealous lover, his imprisonment claimed him even at a distance.

No one had said goodbye to him, some looks, envy, hatred, curiosity; door after door had opened and banged behind him and then he had seen the street, the rows of trees, the movement of traffic and the yellow flatness of the sun on the roofs and fronts of buildings. At the same time as acknowledging that he was free to go the little lawyer had warned him not to go anywhere. But, of course, there *was* nowhere to go.

A letter or two in his fingers from home, messages he could no longer interpret, felt untidy and he got rid of them into a rubbish bin; when they were gone from his touch he felt he wanted them back again; however vaguely, they told him who he was and confirmed himself to himself, but he refused to go back for them, become a Paris down-and-out rummaging in bins; bus-tops with advertisements for *Le Monde,* or impossibly beautiful women in their underclothes; a Métro station, elegant as a grandmother who has become, suddenly, a young girl again, the wrought and carefully-designed ironwork, the steps downwards into a hot flush of sticky noise; people came up, went down, a whirl of feet, legs covered and uncovered, some small calves, some fat, children, tired angry girls with pushcarts, men with briefcases, some North Africans hanging about, young, eyes nervous, watchful, one of them tickled a man's pocket, tossed something to another youth, the two walked off in opposite directions; no concealment, everything in the open, he watched it, witnessed it, and it was as if he were not really there for all they cared. They could spot a man just out of prison and he was the most frightened and useless man on the street.

He walked up to a complex and detailed street-map behind Perspex; ***Vous êtes ICI!*** said a red round circle in its centre. Against a tree someone had tossed an entire, shining white toilet, something from Duchamps, glistening in the sun, brand-new, not a mark; it sat there daring him to make sense of it. He saw the girl's face, the painter's face, streaks of blood like blows from a paintbrush, and passing time was playing tricks, the features were no longer well defined, a short space of time and this is what happened, where was she now? In what hospital? Under guard? If he knew where she was, would he go there? What for?

There was no reason to see her, she was already moving out of the spaces created around him and his ideas about himself. He saw her as if she had been in an erotic photo-album, one black-and-white legs-spread photo among many, and he had thrown the album away. He had a memory of a memory. Why he had acted as he had did not matter and it mattered even less whether she understood. When he would inevitably face her again – the little lawyer was not very precise on this point – they would be altered beyond each other, or anything they had experienced. Nothing – in a frighteningly short time – would be secret or sacred. The world would stare at his opened soul. Yes, too dramatic; he was only an actor now, not the entire play. You had to concede, give in, know things for what they were; the whole business had been sordid, messy, irresponsible, stupid; the mind that had participated in it had been without strengths, real strengths, without parameters, no idea of left or right, while capable of immense self-delusion, perhaps that was merely a way of protecting itself: perhaps it had not even been *his* mind.

He thought about the painter and his dyed-red hair and porcelain face and whether he should go there, back to that yard, the rooms, the paintings of impossible people in histories that existed only in the mind of a dead man. He could not go there – the thought of the place, even the effort at imagining it, made him so frightened that he felt his bowels shift, push, he did not want to foul himself in the street.

He was in a quarter now full of small bright shops, local people, a small park with children and mothers; he sought its small comforts of children's voices and the exuberance or silence of young women. He had no idea what time it was. Another bus passed and the destination sign read Parc des Princes. The children ran about, fell, cried for attention, all that energy, the young mothers sat patiently, as he sat, and across the small park through a clutch of green bushes a 'plane rose as if it were a toy, a thing on a string, silvering into the blue sky. He felt sad, but for a long time he did not move. First one, then another young mother looked over at him, stared. He stood up.

Talking to himself, walking from pavement to pavement, watching the little red men at traffic-lights become little green men; *permissions,* he had to have permission to walk forward in a straight line; he found a café bar and sat down and ordered a black coffee. The waiter didn't even look at him, the coffee sloshed over the edges of the tiny cup, distressing, vulgar, perhaps he smelled, he needed a decent wash, a bath, again he fingered the cards the lawyer had given him, their rough feel; across the street was a flower shop and over its front door an enormous red rose, in appalling neon, blinked and flirted.

He sipped his coffee, his wristwatch had stopped and was now cynically useless, the afternoon peeled another layer off itself, bullying snarl of big vehicles and slippery oiled flash of cyclists; he saw small rooms and his other selves talking, drinking, drunk, opening the world so that he could rearrange it in his own image. He looked around – the rose flicked on, off, on – and felt a new terror; he knew no one, there was not one familiar face passing him by, and he was not familiar to any of them. Invisibility by another name, this not-being-known, this not-being. He had become an *absence.*

There was no single word to describe it. It was like believing in sacraments, or that Christ's flesh inhabited a piece of bread; so terrifying a possibility that it was warm enough to be consoling. Faith had a shape, a texture; like the arc of the painter's brush on a canvas, one had to *believe.* Or the form conversation took floating in the air over tables wet with spilled alcohol, rain on musty windows; it was all too complicated. He should have known. Intelligence had nothing to do with it. Water on water, all that aimless anger. The street swam around him like a shoal of fish, everyone had intention, meaning and direction, the things he lacked or had been emptied of; as if simply sitting and not moving were enough.

The painter's red dyed hair indistinguishable from the daubs of blood kissing his scalp, a snatch of bubbly saliva running into the frame of his trickle of beard had dragged with it daubs of red dye here also, an expression on his face of bewilderment or perhaps discovery, his eyelids parted but no light in his eyes, he was like the unfinished work of a lazy sculptor, his marble face large and seeming to grow even larger, one hand rested its palm against the wall as if he were trying with one last effort to push the wall down; an immensity of spilled blood, the painter's lips parted, mauled stained teeth, shadows gathering in the renewing stains of blood all over him; the stairs as he sat on them, silence in the yard, over the world, a need for action, the girl looking at him as if he had carved her with his own hands out of the air, she was a sketched stained object emerging from one of his notebooks.

There had to be something to *do*. And so, he had unfurled his banner; the real thing, taking such action into oneself, a solitary effort of will, done in a moment, without real preparation, but conclusive, absolute, creating a series of motions which went on and on, knocking into each other and creating even more movement and action, unstoppable, irreversible. Intoxicating, terrifying, the lightness of the move one way or the other, back or forward; a bomb once thrown cannot be immobilised in its flight; the girl had her head in her hands as if she wished to crush it, squeeze out of it everything she saw in front of her and everything she knew, he had reached out and touched her and she had stepped back, up one step, there was blood on her small shoes.

It was more than he could bear; he smoked, he wanted to run to a doctor, beg for something to kill the pain, make him sleep, there was no loneliness in sleep, he wanted to go to the girl, just to see her would be enough, another human being who had been close to him just one in this whole city would be yes enough and no, most certainly he could not do that, things would work out, he was cut off, cut out, he could always write a letter, but to whom? The waiter came out, took away his empty cup. Was this the true nature of freedom – a waiter taking your cup away without a word?

Small ratty birds pecked and darted on clean empty flagstones and in the cantering gutters, like rodents; cries of playing children like the shouts of bathers being drawn further out to sea; clouds breaking apart, tasting sunlight, putting it back on the shelf of Heaven, shopping for the right blend of yellow and gold; a woman in a coat too large and heavy for the day walked a thin flat bone of a dog on a black lead like a thick charcoal line. The day failed to notice him.

He had fallen through himself, a feeling of drowning and nothingness just above the heart, as a ghost must experience when first it realises it has no flesh, no bone, and he sat there smoking, wanting to use the lavatory but afraid to ask, afraid to stand up, to move, discussing this new sensation with himself, his lips working over the words and concepts silently, conscious and careful, knowing that someone going by – and who could tell when, from which direction they would come? – might look into his face and read his lips and know, without any doubt....